Total Eclipse of the Heart

What's a werewolf to do when she finds her soulmate twice? It's a total eclipse of the heart.

It was only a few years ago that humans found out magical creatures existed. Now, they're all out of the closet and leading their lives freely when they once used to hide their true identity. Werewolves, vampires, fairies and everything else that goes bump in the night.

When Lena walks into the Eclipse bar, she turns Rachel's world inside out. She's a werewolf who scents her mate, and nothing will stop her from claiming what's hers.

Rachel has always assumed that when she mated with Jerrod she'd never know another lover, despite her longing for both men and women. No werewolf would be unfaithful. Ever. She's heard of werewolves having two mates in one lifetime, but after the first one died, not at the same time. She's terrified of how the man she loves will react when he finds out the instincts that drew her to him five years ago now pull her to another woman.

This book has been previously published and has been revised and expanded from its original release.

Warning, this title contains the following: Explicit sex, graphic language, anal sex, mild violence, female/female/male interactions, ménage lovin', hot girl-on-girl action and a fisting scene that might make your thighs tingle. Enjoy!

Big Girls Don't Die

"I will always love you." Not just a figure of speech when you're undead.

Six months ago, Andre St. James committed the ultimate one-night-stand party foul by turning Cynthiana into the spawn of Satan...also known as a vampire. He insisted he knew they were meant to be together forever and ever, so why wait for her to be on the same page with him to suck the life out of her?

What. Ever. The only thing the two of them share is chemistry that blasts off the charts. So she dropkicked him out of her life and told him to never come back. He listened. Until now.

Andre knows Cyn has trouble dealing with his take-no-prisoners approach to life, and that turning her against her will was a mistake. But he's got patience born of centuries of immortality, and he'll do whatever it takes to get back into her good graces and stay there forever. Including wait until she has no choice but to turn to him.

After all, no one understands forever like a vampire. He's loved her from the moment he saw her...and he always will.

This book has been previously published and has been revised from its original release.

Warning: Naughty vampire nookie. Orgasmic biting, a little bloodsucking, and a hot tub scene that redefines STEAMY.

It's Raining Men

She loves them too much to change them. Until they turn the tables on her...

Every one of Candy's werewolf instincts tells her that Michael is her mate. He's a lawyer—smart, sophisticated, and handsome. The catch? He's gay. There is no way she's going to try to change who he is. Then she meets his lover Stephen, a seductive Fae-siren jazz singer, and she's positive she's got a screw loose somewhere. Mates with not one, but two gay men?

She's definitely doomed to be single forever.

Michael and Stephen know that their unexpectedly flirtatious advances have thrown Candy for a loop. But there's method to their madness—they're both serious about her. And they plan to make sure she never spends another birthday alone.

Warning: Nekked men doing dirty, dirty things to each other and a very lucky woman, sexy biting of mates, seductive siren singing and a naughty masturbation in a public restroom. Hey, a girl has to do what a girl has to do!

Crazy Little Thing Called Love

Love can drive you over the edge. It can also let you fly.

Pixie Parthon worked hard to make her music production company a success. Anyone who gets in her way gets the business end of her Fae magic. Her savvy business sense kept her family afloat for years, but now that her musician brother is mated and off on a world tour she's feeling left in the dust.

Maybe it was a faint wish for a little love magic for herself, but she didn't expect one night of cutting loose to leave her marked for life. A little love bite is one thing. Give up her hard-won independence to a pushy alpha werewolf? She'll pass.

Malcon is just as shocked as Pixie, but for a different reason. From the moment he saw her, his desire went far beyond getting into her pants. When she agreed—begged—to be bitten, he believed she also sensed their destiny to be mates.

Now it's too late. Nothing will convince Pixie that he has no intention of clipping her wings—not even a month's worth of orgasms on call. Crazy as it sounds, love is all he wants from her. Even if it means letting her go...

Warning: Dirty wolf on fairy love, semi-orgasmic dance scenes, fully orgasmic biting of mates, Alpha males and women who are willing to smack them with fairy dust when they get out of line. Oh, and some hot anal sex. You're welcome!

Look for these titles by *Crystal Jordan*

Now Available:

Treasured

Unbelievable series
If You Believe (Book 1)
Believe in Me (Book 2)
Make Me Believe (Book 3)

In the Heat of the Night series
Total Eclipse of the Heart (Book 1)
Big Girls Don't Die (Book 2)
It's Raining Men (Book 3)
Crazy Little Thing Called Love (Book 4)

Wasteland series
The Wanderer

In the Heat of the Night

Crystal Jordan

A Samhain Publishing, Ltd. publication.

Samhain Publishing, Ltd.
577 Mulberry Street, Suite 1520
Macon, GA 31201
www.samhainpublishing.com

In the Heat of the Night
Print ISBN: 978-1-60504-740-9
Total Eclipse of the Heart Copyright © 2010 by Crystal Jordan
Big Girls Don't Die Copyright © 2010 by Crystal Jordan
It's Raining Men Copyright © 2010 by Crystal Jordan
Crazy Little Thing Called Love Copyright © 2010 by Crystal Jordan

Editing by Bethany Morgan

Total Eclipse of the Heart, ISBN 978-1-60504-208-4
First Samhain Publishing, Ltd. electronic publication: October 2008
Big Girls Don't Die, ISBN 978-1-60504-379-1
First Samhain Publishing, Ltd. electronic publication: February 2009
It's Raining Men, ISBN 978-1-60504-536-8
First Samhain Publishing, Ltd. electronic publication: May 2009
Crazy Little Thing Called Love, ISBN 978-1-60504-625-9
First Samhain Publishing, Ltd. electronic publication: July 2009
First Samhain Publishing, Ltd. print publication: June 2010

Contents

Total Eclipse of the Heart

Dedication

For R.G. Alexander, because she got me an awesome editor and because she deserved a heroine of her own. The hot werewolf nookie is just a bonus.

And for Bethany Morgan, editor extraordinaire. Thanks for putting your money where your mouth is and believing in my work enough to buy it. You rock!

Chapter One

I watched my husband leer at another woman's breasts. The woman—a werewolf named Candy—was stacked. Just the kind of girl I used to shag before I met my mate. Jerrod's rich laugh reached my ears and made me smile. It was a game to flirt with our customers at Eclipse. A game we played well.

Eclipse was *the* nightspot for things that went bump in the night. Things any smart human didn't want to bump into. Ever.

As a werewolf, I was one of those things. And so was my mate.

"Hi, Rachel!"

"Hey, Cole, Marty, Frank." I nodded to some of my regular patrons as I passed, putting an extra swing in my hips because I knew they'd stare at my ass as I walked by. They should at least get a good show, right? All three of them were fairies...and by fairies, I didn't mean the kind that dug on other men. I meant the kind who had to tuck in their wings to get a shirt over their heads.

I took a deep breath, letting the familiarity of the bar wrap around me. The splashes of noise from people and music. Perfect. I'd worked my whole life to get this kind of stability and routine. It was something my mother had never provided while I was growing up—but my mate had, and I loved the man more than life itself for it. He made damn sure I had everything I needed and then some. We'd made a crazy success of Eclipse in the four years since we'd opened our doors. He wanted to expand and open a second club, but change was something I always resisted. Things were so fantastic right now, why mess with a good thing? A wry grin pulled at my lips. It would probably take him another six months of showing me business plans and financial projections before I gave in and agreed. I shook my head and sighed.

Winding my way from the stockroom to the bar, I carried two cases of domestic beer behind the sleek black counter. My werewolf strength made it easy to bear the load, something that wouldn't have been possible for a human woman. I set the cases out of the way and dusted off my gray top and short leather skirt. Glancing up, I smiled at Cynthiana Trent. She and Candy often came to Eclipse—probably because it wasn't kosher for the leggy vampire to have a werewolf as her best friend, but my mate wouldn't let anyone hassle them. Eclipse was neutral territory and anyone who broke that rule got their ass handed to them by Jerrod as he showed them to the door. The werewolf pack leaders weren't all that pleased that we served vampires, but so far we hadn't given them any reason to meddle in our business.

Vampires and werewolves had hated each other for centuries. It wasn't until a few years ago that we'd all come out of the closet about what we were and let humans in on our hairy little secret. It was the escalation of fighting that made us public—and because of that, we'd outted all the other magical creatures with us. I'd never gotten involved in the conflict, but vampires were a weird lot. Anyone who lived forever just could not be normal. I was happy with the couple hundred years I'd get as a werewolf.

While I stepped up to the bar, an enormous vampire approached Cyn, and she offered him a fuck-off-and-die look.

The man was gorgeous, all chocolate skin and pale green eyes. Still not as attractive as Jerrod, but then, no vampire could compare to a full-blooded werewolf. I knew it was a prejudiced thought, but he was my man. I could be biased if I wanted to.

"Hey, lover." I wound my arms around Jerrod from behind, kissing the mated bite mark on his bare left shoulder. My bite mark. He often tended bar without his shirt on, so I was surprised into laughter when he turned in my embrace and I saw he was wearing a bow tie.

"Hey, yourself."

"You look like a Chippendale dancer." A giggle bubbled up in my throat.

He gripped my hips, pulling me closer so I could feel his erection. "Just wanted to give you something to unwrap for our anniversary. Since you have to work tonight."

"Only for another hour, then Benny will take over for us." A slow smile pulled at my lips as heat exploded through me. Just like that I was wet for him, wanting him. It was always that way between werewolf mates. Hotter, stronger, better than it could be with anyone else. God, I loved him. Needed him. Right now. I eyed the long bar, wondering for a moment if our customers would mind if we put on a little show for them. Five minutes, that was all I'd need. Two even.

His midnight blue gaze raked down my body, taking in the beaded nipples that stood out against the thin material of my top. He shook his head, a hot predatory gleam in his eyes. "You'll have to wait, Rach."

"Damn." I squeezed my thighs together, willing the relentless ache to subside. It didn't. Swallowing back a helpless whimper, I arched my hips against him to rub myself on his thick cock.

His big hands stilled my hips, fingers tightening when I tried to move. "You don't want to play that game."

"Don't I?" I licked my lips, desire winding through me as his gaze followed the motion.

"No." His fingers slipped up to clench in my long dark hair, pulling my head back. Dipping forward, he nudged my shirt aside to expose my collarbone. And the bite he'd marked me with five years ago. He closed his mouth over the mark, sucking hard.

My back bowed hard as a lightning flash of pleasure arced from the mark to my dampening pussy. I gasped, my fingers curling into claws on his shoulders. His tongue flicked over the mark again and again until my mouth opened in a silent scream as my pussy fisted on nothing. The fire inside me built until I couldn't stand it, and I bit my lip to keep from crying out. My eyes squeezed closed as I shook apart in his arms, orgasm exploding deep within me.

"Ahem." Someone cleared his throat, interrupting us.

Jerrod's hands cupped my elbows as he set me away from him. The fog of lust cleared from my brain, but slowly. My God, what had I just done? At *work*? The only thing that blocked me from the view of our customers was Jerrod's broad chest. Heat flooded my cheeks, and I locked my knees to remain upright. Every werewolf in the place would have been able to smell me getting off.

While Jerrod turned to serve our interrupter, I bent behind the bar to pretend to straighten the strap on my high heel.

"You all right?" He glanced down at me while he mixed a Bloody Mary.

"Fine. You had to take it that far?"

He chuckled. "You wanted to play."

I leaned in and bit him behind the knee, nipping him through his pinstriped trousers. He jerked in surprise. "Don't think I'm done playing, lover."

A grin quirked his full lips, wicked promise flashing in his gaze before he turned away again. I shivered, thinking of all the things he might do to me.

This would be an anniversary to remember.

Chapter Two

My hand shook as I slid a frosty glass and a bottle of Corona onto a small round table. Unease wound through me, and I didn't know why. The feeling skittered up my back and made my skin crawl. I knew this feeling, but I couldn't place it. Some instinct within me was kicking into high gear and I was drawing a big fat blank as to what I was supposed to be getting. It was damned annoying, and inconvenient. I woke this morning to a lead ball in my stomach, and it had only gotten worse all day. I'd done everything I could to ignore it, to hide it from Jerrod, but it hadn't helped.

"Thanks, Rachel."

"No problem." I tucked my hair behind my ear and flicked another glance around the bar. The place was packed, but that was normal. Everything appeared...normal. So why couldn't I shake this feeling? I rolled my shoulders to try and ease the tension.

Fifteen more minutes and I'd be off for the night. I could drag Jerrod upstairs to our big apartment and let him screw my brains out. I'd wake tomorrow and everything would be fine. It had to be or I was going to go nuts. Rubbing my temple, I tried to massage away a headache that began to form.

"It hurts because you're fighting it."

The woman's voice had a whiskey kick to it, soft and rough at the same time. I spun to face her, *needing* to see the person attached to that voice. Werewolf definitely, I could smell the wolf on her. She had the smoothest cocoa skin I'd ever seen. Her black hair fell in a riot of curls around her face and emphasized her ebony eyes. They were fathomless, beautiful. They drew me in, and I stepped toward her. Our gazes locked, heated and my heart lurched. All the instincts I'd been suppressing today jumped up to bite me in the ass. Something snapped inside my chest, some deep pull of recognition.

Mate.

"No," I gasped the word, stumbling back and lifting my tray like it was a shield. Shock roared through me. My heart squeezed, and I couldn't breathe. Oh God. Oh. God.

"Yes." Possession flashed hot in her gaze. "I'm Lena." She stepped forward, reaching for me.

And I wanted her to touch me, stroke me. Lust twisted inside me, fire licking my veins. *No.* I turned and fled for the stockroom. Jerrod would *kill* me. How could this happen? Was it even possible? I'd heard of werewolves having two mates in one lifetime before, but after the first mate *died*, not *at the same time.* No one would believe this was possible, especially not other werewolves. But, there was no denying what I felt. It was just like the first time I'd met Jerrod, the instantaneous kick to the heart and loin. Everything inside me wanted her. To know her, to love her, to *possess* her.

"Oh God," I breathed. My stomach pitched, and my palms grew slick. Clamping a hand over my mouth, I fought back the need to vomit. What was I going to do? I couldn't lose Jerrod. Infidelity was unheard of among my kind. Matings were for life, forever. Jerrod was my mate, my everything. A soul mate fashioned just for me.

So was Lena.

Stomping down on the inner voice, I leaned against the wall and bent to stick my head between my knees. The tray slipped from my fingers and dropped to the floor. My heart hammered against my ribs as all the blood rushed to my head. I just needed to *breathe*, to think clearly.

Being bisexual, I never thought I'd have just one person forever, but life was full of surprises. And Jerrod was the best thing that had ever happened to me. I couldn't fuck this up. Fisting my fingers in my hair, I pressed on my skull in an attempt to ease the shrieking pain. The need to mate was there, ripping into me with the fierce jaws of the wolf within.

I sucked in a deep breath and pulled Lena's scent to me. Somehow, I already knew it. It was imbedded in my psyche already, just like Jerrod's. Just her smell was enough to make me want, make me wet. The muscles in my thighs locked, shaking with the need to go to her. Tears pressed against my lids. *Jerrod.* Where was he? I needed his steady strength. But Lena was out there, between me and my mate.

The door to the stockroom swung open and then closed with a solid *thunk*.

It was her. Lena. I didn't need to look up to know. My instincts cried out in recognition, rioting within me. My nipples tightened, my pussy dampening with the hot need to claim and be claimed. *No.* Please, no. I dug my nails into my scalp, welcoming the pain. Anything to distract me from the pulsing want clawing at my flesh.

"Why do you run?"

My mind scrabbled for any excuse to make her leave. "You can't be in here. Staff only."

The heat from her body enveloped me as she stepped closer. I snapped upright, pressing my back against the wall. There was no escape. I couldn't get away. I didn't want to. My breath panted out, logic and instinct warring inside me. I closed my eyes, trying to shut out the inevitable.

"Rachel." Her breath fanned against my ear.

I moaned. The sound of my name in that husky voice made my body ache with lust. "How do you know my name?"

"That's what the men you served called you, isn't it?"

"Yes."

"*Yesssss.*" She flicked her tongue against my neck.

I shuddered, molten heat rolling through me. I was so wet I couldn't stand it. My legs felt too weak to hold me up. I tilted my head back, swallowing hard. My breath bellowed out.

Her hand lifted to cover my breast, tweaking the tight nipple. A soft cry ripped from my throat. I arched into her caress, lust clouding my mind. Nothing mattered right now but the mating ritual, taking what was mine. I needed it—her. Now.

Jerrod's face flashed through my mind. I couldn't *do* this. I couldn't hurt him that way. I couldn't.

I stepped sideways, but she shoved me against the wall. Her hand dropped to my leg, slipping under my short skirt.

"Stop." I arched my torso, fighting her. Fighting myself.

"No." She rubbed her palm over my panties. The heel of her hand hit my swollen clit. I sobbed, my hips twisting. It only increased the friction. She thrust her fingers under the scrap of lace, plunging them into my pussy.

"*Please.*" But I didn't know what I was begging for anymore. For her to stop. For her to never stop. My hips jerked, and I ground my pussy against her plunging fingers. I felt a drop of my wetness trail down my leg. My thighs shook, and I gasped as her hand worked me, pushing me closer and closer to orgasm.

A satisfied smile curved her lips, triumph shining in her midnight eyes. "You're mine. You'll always be mine."

Crystal Jordan

"Yes. *No.* Stop. Please, stop." She had to stop. I didn't have the strength to make her. My body shook with need, feral heat exploding in my belly. The wolf inside me howled, wanting to seize my mate.

"Why?"

Why? For a moment, I didn't know. I wanted what she wanted. Everything inside me screamed for it. I threw my head back, smacking hard against the wall. Stars exploded behind my eyelids. The pain brought a small return of sanity.

"I can't do this. I'm already mate—"

The door snapped open, and Jerrod walked in. He froze, his eyes widening at the sight of his mate with another woman. Oh. Shit. My heart lurched, and ice water rushed through my veins. Cold sweat broke out on my forehead. I clenched my fingers, trying to still their sudden shaking.

No. Oh, no.

"Jerrod," I gasped. "I-it's not what it looks like."

"Isn't it?" Rage darkened his gaze. His big body hummed with tension as he stalked forward. One hand wrapped around Lena's biceps, wrenching her away from me. My body screamed in protest, and I arched toward her.

He pulled Lena around to face him. "That is *my* mate."

"And mine." Her chin jutted in stubborn defiance.

"Liar." He snarled, his nose nearly touching hers. Then his jaw went slack, and he jerked back as though he'd been burned. "No."

Lena stiffened, and I could feel her shock. "Mate."

Her eyes flicked to me, then back to Jerrod. She swallowed, shifting in her tall black boots.

Jerrod shook his head, pressing the heel of his hand to his forehead. His breath hissed out. "How is this possible?"

22

Lena licked her lips. "I don't—I don't know. I just know what I feel."

"You can't—"

She lifted her hand to cup his cheek. "My mate."

For the first time in five years, I saw Jerrod speechless. He went rigid, uncertainty flashing in his eyes. He glanced at me. "Rachel?"

The words jerked out. Please let this be the right thing to say. Fear shook me to my very core, twisting tight in my belly. "I feel it too. With you. With her. Mate."

He pulled back, stepping away from Lena...and me. Pain ripped through me, stabbing deep into my heart. This was it. I would lose him, and the separation would drive us both to madness. A sob lodged in my throat, clogging my airway.

"Ladies first." A smile flashed across his handsome face. He settled against the door, arms folding across his wide chest.

I blinked, torn between hope and utter shock. It was going to be all right. Relief flooded me. Could it really be that easy? My eyes squeezed closed. I wouldn't lose Jerrod. A rough shudder rippled through me. I needed him so much. Loved him. Craved him. Couldn't live without him. Our gazes met, and understanding shone in his eyes. He knew what this meant to me. Of course he did. He knew me as no other ever could. Except Lena.

Lena's smoky laugh floated in the long room. "You want to watch...Jerrod?"

"Yes." He glanced between us, a wolfish grin on his lips.

I licked my lips. "Jerrod, are you—"

"Don't worry, Rach. I'm next." His indigo eyes heated, caressing me.

Lena turned to me, pressing me back against the wall. This time I didn't resist. I cupped her hips in my palms, pulling her to me. We both moaned as our bodies met for the first time. I bent forward to catch her mouth with mine. She slid her hands in my hair, and I shuddered as she stroked through the length. Goose bumps erupted on my arms. I tilted my head, moving my lips slowly over hers and savoring this first moment between us. She opened her mouth to suckle my bottom lip. She nipped my lip, a sweet sting. I moaned, desire raging hot and wild through me. She called to me, this woman. I needed her.

Sliding my hands around, I gripped her ass. Wedging my knee between her thighs, I pressed her sex to my leg. She wore no underpants under her short, pleated skirt. I could feel the wetness of her hot pussy as she rode my thigh, her hips arching against me. Over her shoulder, I met Jerrod's gaze. I shivered at the fire burning there. He loved this, I could tell. He lightly stroked his cock through his slacks as he watched us.

"Rachel." Her breath panted against my lips, and I smiled because I could do this to her.

Her head tilted back as her hips moved on my leg. I flexed the muscles, pushing deeper to work over her swollen clit. Lifting a hand to her full breast, I pinched the beaded nipple through her black top. She gasped.

Now. Mark her. Make her mine. Forever.

Instinct roared through me, untamed, uncontrolled. Feral wolf. Leaning forward, I bit her exposed throat. She jolted against me, screaming. The sweet nectar of her blood flooded my tongue. I felt her pussy jerk spasmodically as she came apart in my arms. I sucked at her throat, licking the bite as it healed. She shuddered and moaned, her hips snapping forward in short, slamming thrusts.

Through it all, I felt Jerrod's eyes upon us. It was hotter because he watched. The smell of his desire reached my nose.

Wetness flooded my pussy, and I moaned deep in my throat. My hips twisted in unrelenting want. For my mates. Both of them. Harsh emotion banded my chest at the thought. Yes. Possession, need...and love warred for dominance. My eyes squeezed closed.

Lena's arms wrapped around me, her face burying into my shoulder. I stroked her ebony curls, holding her close. I remembered what it was like to mate the first time, the overwhelming flood of emotion, connection. She trembled against me, her breath puffing across the skin of my neck.

"Lena."

Her tongue flicked out to lick me. "Yes, mate?"

"Finish it." Yes. I wanted to be claimed.

She pulled back, slipping her hand up to cup my cheek. "Not so fast."

"Now."

"As you wish." Bending forward, she sucked my nipple into her mouth. She pressed the tip to the top of her mouth, biting down. The cloth of my shirt rubbed against the sensitive flesh.

Heat rushed through me, and I arched toward her hot, wet mouth. She moved to my other breast, nipping the crest. My hands clenched in her soft hair as I tried to pull her closer. Desperation whipped through me. The need for her, the need to mate, the need for fast, hard orgasm.

"Lena, please. I want...more."

Her fingers pressed between my legs and I relaxed my thighs to allow her access. She thrust two fingers into me. A hard, harsh push.

"*Yes.*"

I twined my fingers with her free hand, clenching tight. Hot shivers streaked through me, the rising tide of orgasm jerking me forward. I rocked against her fingers, loving the feel of her within me.

She lifted my hand to her mouth, kissing the center of my palm. I trembled. Our gazes locked, and her eyes burned to a translucent blue. She was close to feral, the wolf breaking loose. Opening her mouth on my wrist, she bit down hard. Claiming me. I screamed, my body jolting under the sensation, and I flashed over into sudden orgasm.

"*Lena.*"

She laved the bite mark again and again, drawing out the feelings and pushing me hard against the edge of sanity.

Tears burned my eyes, spilling over to slip down my cheeks. Sweet relief swirled through me. Yes. This was perfect. The pain and dread that rode me all day fell away into nothingness. A connection that could never be broken spun between us. It was so right, so good.

A sharp knock sounded on the door, making me jerk in surprise. Benny's voice rang through, "Hey, boss."

Jerrod stepped aside, cracking the door open. He exchanged soft words with the other man, and then closed it again.

He flicked a glance over his shoulder, a knowing grin tugging at his lips. "I—uh, think we need to take this upstairs."

Chapter Three

"You moved to Los Angeles recently?" I asked the question as we walked up the steps to the apartment. I could feel both their gazes burning into my back.

When I reached the top landing, I turned to punch the access code into a keypad mounted beside the door. My hands shook so badly I had to concentrate on a task that was almost second nature. The locks clicked back.

This was it. Letting someone enter our wolf den was huge. I sucked in a deep breath, trying to settle my nerves. Everything had changed in a blink of an eye. And now that the storm had passed I was freaking out. *Two* mates. Oh my holy Jesus. Breathe. Just breathe. That was the key here.

"Yes. How did you know?" I heard the surprise in Lena's voice.

Laughing, I glanced back at her. "No one lives in L.A. long without coming to Eclipse. And this is definitely your first time here."

"Yeah. I-I was in Phoenix and just decided to move a few weeks ago. It was sudden."

"Instinct?" Reaching around both of us, Jerrod pushed open the door to our apartment.

She sighed. "At the time I thought I was crazy, but now...it makes sense."

"You were drawn to us." We walked in, and I went straight for the kitchen. Wine. I needed something to settle me. Deep breathing wasn't cutting it. I was about to hyperventilate. My heels clicked on the gleaming hardwood floor. Jerrod and I had spent a whole year restoring the upper story of the warehouse that housed Eclipse. It was all worth it, the place was gorgeous. And the commute couldn't be beat.

Lena followed me and wandered about, touching this and that. She stroked a finger over the marble countertops. Curiosity shone in her gaze as she looked at everything. What did she see when she entered our den? I was afraid she wouldn't approve. There was so much we didn't know about each other. But we were mated.

I rounded the island, stooping to pluck up a bottle of Cabernet Sauvignon. *Get a grip, Rachel.* So many emotions crashed through me I wasn't sure how to react. I wanted Lena here, but how would it affect Jerrod and me? And I felt selfish and ashamed for even thinking it.

Jerrod snagged the wine bottle from my trembling fingers over the kitchen island. His steady gaze met mine. "You're worried."

That was Jerrod. A man of few words who cut right to the chase. He was my rock. "Yes."

"You think the werewolf pack leaders will have a problem with our mating?"

Um. No. The thought hadn't even occurred to me yet. Shit. I bit my lip and tried not to have a mild mental meltdown. We weren't exactly a werewolf pack leader favorite, and this could really fuck us up. "It is a concern."

Jerrod shook his head. "One for another time."

"No. It's not a concern." Lena walked up beside me, her arms crossing over her chest.

I sighed. "It's not that simple."

She shook her head firmly, eyebrows raising. "I just found you. Both of you. I won't give that up so easily. Not because someone is too narrow-minded to see how right it is. Instinct pulled me to you. And I'm staying, damn it."

Stubborn. A good word to describe my new mate. A good word to describe both of my mates. It was going to be fun to see the two of them butt heads. I grinned, forcing myself to think of something besides the possible scrutiny of werewolf pack leaders. Lena was a much more gratifying subject.

"So...what do you do?"

Her arms slid around my waist, pressing her body to mine. Her soft breasts pillowed against my side. I closed my eyes and swallowed, a lightning strike of pleasure flashing through me. My pussy heated, dampened in anticipation. I dragged in a deep breath, trying to quell the rising excitement, but I pulled in Jerrod's scent. Hot, masculine. Mine. Both of them. Mine.

"I'm an electrician."

"W-what?"

"I'm an electrician." She laughed. "I could light up your world, baby."

Jerrod snorted. "Does that line actually work on people?"

She pulled away from me to face him. A slow grin bloomed on her lips as she reached out to run a fingertip down his bare chest. "Did it work on you?"

His gaze heated as he looked down at her, but he said nothing. Stepping around the island, he snaked an arm around her waist, and he spun her back to the cold stainless steel refrigerator. She gasped, arching against him. I knew what that look in his eye meant, he was going to...yes. His lips moved over hers, slow and hot. He bracketed her jaw with his fingers.

Desire twisted through me. I expected to feel jealous, seeing my man with someone else, but I just...didn't. It was like a missing piece had slid into place for me. A hole I didn't even know was there had been filled. And watching them—God, it turned me on.

Palming her breasts, he flicked his fingers over her hard nipples. She moaned into his mouth. Heat exploded through me, and I leaned a hand against the island to stay upright. Kissing his way down her body, he knelt before her. He glanced at me, a small grin on his lips. Tipping his head with a wink, he invited me to join them.

Hooking her knee over his shoulder, he shoved her skirt up and out of the way. Her fingers fisted in his hair. Licking the smooth flesh of her thigh, he opened his mouth on the corded muscles. His gaze met mine, the irises turning a pale, icy blue. Then he bit down.

"Jerrod!" Lena screamed, her body arching as she came. I leaned forward to catch the sound in my mouth.

I thrust my tongue between her lips, joining our mouths. Her kiss was frenzied, desperate. Tangling my hand in her hair, I held her still while I stroked the fingers of my other hand over the mate bite on her neck. She quivered, whimpering against my lips.

Her fingers fumbled with the front of my shirt before slipping down to thrust between my legs. Now it was my turn to moan as she worked her fingertips over my swollen clit through my panties. I caressed her bite mark in time with her strokes. Her hips bucked as Jerrod licked between her thighs.

Oh God. My panties were soaked. Her fingers were touching me just right. She froze, shuddering as she came. Her back arched as I raked my nails across her mate mark. She went limp, collapsing into Jerrod's arms. I sighed, squeezing my thighs together to try and suppress the unrequited lust that still burned there.

Jerrod rose to his feet, licking his lips and grinning down at Lena. His arms encircled both of us, and a moment of sweet silence surrounded us. I relaxed, resting my cheek against his chest. My gaze met Lena's and we shared a smile.

I glanced up and laughed.

His eyebrow arched. "What?"

Reaching up, I snagged his bowtie and untied it. "Happy anniversary, lover."

Using the sides of the bowtie, I pulled him down for a long kiss. I could taste Lena on his lips and I moaned. God, the mingled flavor of them was sweet on my tongue. His soft hair prickled against my palm when I slid my hands into the short black strands.

Lena lifted one of my hands away from him and brought it to her lips. Her tongue licked the mated mark on my wrist. I moaned, arching hard against Jerrod. Liquid heat flooded my pussy. Wrapping my leg around his, my hips molded to his. His hands cupped my backside, lifting me into his thrusts. The cloth of his slacks felt rough against my thighs. I threw my head back, my breath bellowing out of starved lungs.

"Please. Please. Please." I don't know which one of them I was begging, but I wanted...I needed...*please.*

My body twisted under the dual lashes of pleasure. I couldn't take it. I couldn't. My back bowed hard as I came. I squeezed my eyes shut and tears leaked down my cheeks.

Lena drew me away from him and over to the island, running her hands under my top to ease it over my head. I wasn't wearing a bra, so my breasts were now bare. They beaded tight under her gaze. She jerked her top off and dropped it to the floor. Her breasts were gorgeous. I wanted to suck the dark tips into my mouth. I stepped forward, and she wrapped her arms around me, her hands stroking down my back. I moaned as our naked skin made contact. She reached behind me to unzip my skirt, and I did the same for her. Shifting her torso, she rubbed our breasts together, and building excitement flashed through me at the friction.

Using her werewolf strength, she pushed me away and lifted me onto the icy marble surface. My breath hissed out in surprise at the contrast against my overheating skin. Hooking a finger in Jerrod's belt loop, she pulled him to us. Looking into his eyes, she rubbed his straining erection. He groaned as she freed his cock from his pants, pumping him between her fingers. Shoving his slacks down, he kicked them and his shoes aside to stand naked before me. God, he was a beautiful man.

Lena stepped back and pushed him toward me. "Fuck her."

"What?" My eyebrows rose.

Grinning, she ran a finger over Jerrod's shoulders as she stepped around him. "It's my turn to watch."

"You can't see from back there."

"The view from here is just fine, thanks." She laughed as her palms came around to stroke his nipples.

He groaned, closing his big hands around my knees and spreading me wide. I leaned back on my hands for leverage as I lifted my hips. He thrust deep, and I moaned. God, he was huge. The fit was so tight and the angle was perfect as he moved in me. He ground his hips into mine, and I watched Lena's hands stroke over his chest from behind. I clenched my inner muscles on his cock, milking him as he worked his shaft inside me. Pleasure burned in his gaze as he looked at me. I loved it, that we could do this to him, make it better for him. Every push of his cock shoved me closer to orgasm. We moved together faster and faster, harder and harder until I wanted to scream with it. I bit my lip to keep the sound back—only our harsh breathing could be heard. Hot pleasure washed through me, building in waves. Tingles shivered over my flesh. I was so close, so very close to the edge. One of his hands lifted to brush over the mate mark on my collarbone. It was enough. My thighs tensed as I came so hard that for a moment I saw starbursts.

He bent over me to suck my nipples deep in his mouth, drawing out my pleasure. I could see Lena behind him. Her eyes flashed pale blue. She leaned forward and sank her teeth into his right shoulder. Satisfaction thrummed through me at the sight. The circle was complete. Each mated to the other. Bound. Now he would have twin marks—one on each shoulder. Lena's and mine.

He shuddered as he pumped into me, slamming hard. Lena ground his nipples between her fingers, licking both his mate bites until he groaned long and loud. His hips jerked in a hard, frantic rhythm until he froze, his heat flooding me as he came. He braced his hands on either side of my hips, head bowed as he sucked in great gulping breaths. The muscles in his arms shook.

A satisfied smile tugged at his lips when he finally leveraged himself upright. "Well, girls, I think it's past your bedtime."

Lena chuckled. "Don't even think for a second I'm about to start calling you Big Daddy."

"Please. Don't give him any ideas. It's taken me five years of work to get him this nice." I rolled my eyes at her as I slid off the island.

She yawned. "Looks like I showed up at just the right time then."

Jerrod led us to the bedroom. We settled on the big bed, tangling together in a heap. Quiet filled the room as we held each other. It left me with time to think, and a stab of fear pierced me as Jerrod's words ricocheted through my mind.

Was he right? Would the werewolf pack leaders contest our unusual mating? We knew what we were to each other, but would others of our kind understand? Jerrod and I made our living on the business of werewolves. If we were officially Ostracized—I shuddered, closing my eyes. Oh God. We could lose everything we'd worked for. Eclipse would have to close, and that would be it.

No.

I refused to think that way. They had to accept. We would convince them...somehow. They couldn't deny our instincts, no more than we could. It wouldn't be easy, but time would only make our new bond stronger, deeper. Right?

"I'm so glad I found you." Lena's husky whisper reached my ears. I didn't know if she spoke to Jerrod or me. It didn't matter.

Jerrod licked the bite mark on my collarbone in a long, slow swipe, making me shiver. His hand stroked up and down my belly. "Me too. Stop worrying, Rach. This isn't something you can solve tonight. We'll make it through this."

"I'm glad we're together. All of us." I closed my eyes, knowing Jerrod was right. We couldn't fix this tonight, couldn't change how others would react to us. But we could strengthen our new bond as much as possible tonight. I grinned. Oh, yes. We could definitely do that. Starting right now.

Chapter Four

Pounding on the door woke me the next morning. I groaned and tried to roll over, but I was sandwiched between my mates, and I couldn't move. The pounding continued. "I'm *coming*."

Fuck. Didn't people know not to wake a bartender before dusk? Jerrod had shifted into his wolf form sometime during the night, so a large timber wolf pressed up against one side of me. Lena lay on her belly, legs akimbo and half off the mattress. I shimmied the other way. Throwing my leg over Jerrod, I deliberately elbowed him in the side as I flopped out of bed. If I had to be awake, he damn well better be too. He snorted and rolled to his back, his paws dangling in the air. Jerking on a robe, I tightened the belt before I poked his muzzle. Hard. "Someone's at the door. Get. Up."

He sighed and stretched, a sound similar to a hundred knuckles popping in rapid succession filling the room as he shifted into his human form. I shivered at the noise—as many times as I'd heard it, it still grossed me out. He groaned and rubbed a palm down his face. "Shit."

"Tell me about it." Lena pushed herself up on her hands and knees. "Who the hell is banging on the door at dawn?"

Rolling to his feet, Jerrod took a breath, his gaze sharpening to a killing edge. "Alain."

The head watchdog of the werewolf pack leaders. He had the air of a sleazy lawyer that sent chills down my spine every time he came into Eclipse for a drink. If he'd been sent by the pack leaders, then it was serious. Oh God. With a snap of their fingers, we could be Ostracized, *persona non grata*. In a word— screwed. No wolf in their right mind would come to Eclipse if we were thrown out of the pack, and no other magical creature was stupid enough to stick around someone the pack leaders might declare open war on at any moment. No matter how any of them felt about us personally, they had no interest in a family feud.

We could lose everything. Have to flee and hope to hell another pack would take us. A million scenarios bounced through my head, each uglier and more devastating than the last.

"They're here faster than I thought." All the blood drained out of my face, and I swayed on my feet. A small part of me had hoped they'd never come.

Through it all, the steady pounding on the door continued. I hadn't had much hope that Alain would give up and go away, but that ceaseless knock killed it. My heart hammered in slow, sick dread while my stomach turned somersaults. Nausea built in the back of my throat, and I stared at my two mates for a long moment while they both threw on some clothes. What would the pack leaders do to us?

Jerrod stalked out into the living room and jerked the door open. His voice held only the barest hint of courtesy when he spoke. "Alain."

The tall, slim man stepped into our home like he owned it, and I barely held back a snarl. No matter how I felt about him, he was a man with power whom I couldn't afford to piss off. Damn it.

"So, you're the interloper." His gaze raked over Lena and then transferred to me. Revulsion flooded me.

I watched the muscles of Jerrod's body go rigid. He stepped between Alain and us. "What do you want, Alain?"

"I would hope you're smart enough to figure that out, Jerrod. Alas, I see I overestimated your intelligence. Pity." He straightened the cuffs on his French blue shirt. "Word of your unconventional new mating has reached the pack leaders. Malcon *requests* the two of you come before him for a ruling on this matter."

Malcon, the pack Alpha. He was a new leader, and no one knew much about him—not even me. And that was saying something, because I was a bartender, and the only person to receive more confessions than a priest was someone in my line of business. Every piece of gossip always made it back to Eclipse, to me. All I knew was that our pack's old Alpha, Malcon's father, had died a few months ago. The pack still waited to see how Malcon's leadership would differ from his father's. He'd been a quiet heir, never a hint of scandal, never stepping so much as a toe out of line. And never giving any hint of his own leanings on how he'd rule the pack. That could be good for us. Or very bad. If he was as conservative as dear old dad—or more so—then we were pooch screwed.

"What about me? The *interloper's* presence isn't required?" Lena propped her hands on her hips, glaring at the slimy bastard.

"You're no one to us. Yet. *If* the pack leaders should rule in your favor, you would still need to approach the Alpha to be accepted into the pack." His condescending look said how unlikely that was.

A harsh growl tore from Jerrod's throat. "Careful how you talk to my mate."

"W-we'll see if she's actually your mate." But all the color leeched out of the other man's face, and he turned to flee without looking back.

"Coward," Lena hissed, stomping over to slam the door behind him with enough force to rip it off its hinges. "Jackass fucktard."

"Careful." I didn't know if I was talking about the door or about how loudly she spoke. Alain might have heard her, and no matter how big of a prick he was, he still had the ear of the Alpha. Jerrod could get away with more because he was already a member of the pack. Lena couldn't afford to push her luck. Our luck.

She rounded on me, fire flickering in her gaze. "What do you care? We could just leave. We don't have to stay where some *cowardly jackass fucktard* tries to tell us who we're able to mate to. That's instinct. Everyone knows wolves can't control that. It's destiny."

"I care because this is our *life* you're talking about. We can't just leave—we have roots here." Roots I'd waited my whole life to put down. Too much change, too fast. It whirled around me, and I wanted to vomit. It was just like when I was growing up. Everything went just fine until one day *bam*, the other shoe dropped and all my stability went sucking out from under my feet like sand in a riptide.

Tossing her hair over her shoulder, she arched a brow. Her voice took on a haughty edge. "Well, we can't stay if they won't let me in the pack. That Alain guy made it sound like that will be a major problem with *your* Alpha. In Phoenix, we had a more open-minded Alpha."

Anger sparked through me at her words, at the whole situation. Terror followed in its wake to streak through me at the upheaval that had become my life in the blink of an eye. We stood to lose everything we'd ever worked for. Eclipse. Our home. My hands shook at the thought, and bitterness coated my tongue. She just walked into the middle of all of it and took over. I crossed my arms over my chest and narrowed my eyes at her. "That's easy for you to say. You can't just sweep in and change everything. And we wouldn't even *have* a problem with Alain or any of the pack leaders if—"

I slapped a hand over my lips to cut myself off before I finished that ugly, awful thought, but it was too late. Mates were a gift, something not every wolf got. And I had two and had just spoken as though I didn't want one of them—it was obvious Lena was here because of *me*, because I was bisexual—Jerrod's sexuality didn't call for anything except women. Oh, shit. What had I done? Jerrod's mouth had dropped open, and he stared at me as if I'd sprouted horns.

But Lena's reaction was worse. Her face went ashen and tears rose in her dark eyes. She swallowed and finished the sentence for me. "If I hadn't shown up to ruin your perfect life? Thanks, Rachel. Thanks so much. You think this is *easy* for me, coming in last? The third wheel? The pack leaders think I don't belong—and you *agree* with them? How the hell do you think I feel?"

I held out my hands, horrified that I'd done something to damage the fragile emotional bonds that formed between new mates. "That wasn't what I meant. I didn't—"

She spun on her heel and walked out the door without stopping to put on her shoes. She was just...gone. I staggered sideways, feeling gutted. I was such an idiot. Oh God.

"Well, this is going to be fun." Jerrod caught me and lead me to the loveseat in the corner.

I turned to fist my fingers in his T-shirt, desperate for him to believe me. Tears blurred my vision. "Jerrod, I'm so sorry. I would never think that about either of you. It just came out all wrong."

"I know, Rach. All the changes and upheaval freaked you out. I get that. But *she* doesn't." His warm gaze met mine, understanding and irritation flashing in their depths. It was a look I was used to. "She doesn't know either of us, how we think, how we operate."

"And it's harder for her because we do know that stuff about each other. I know. I *know*. I'm such an ass." I flopped down on the sofa, burying my face in my hands. Now I had even more problems to figure out, and these ones were my own damn fault. What a huge, cluster-fucked mess.

Chapter Five

As much as I wanted to go after Lena, Jerrod insisted we had to answer the summons of the werewolf pack leaders first. So we drove downtown to reach the skyscraper that housed the pack leader headquarters. It was also an international business, but for those of us in the pack, it was where the movers and shakers could be found. And faced the way we had to now.

Worry gnawed at me. Not just for this meeting, but because of what my words had done to my mate. Lena. I'd messed up badly, and I had no idea how I was going to fix it. I hadn't dealt with another woman in a relationship for the better part of a decade. If Jerrod or I said the wrong thing, we called each other on it and handled the issue. End of story. There was no walking away.

A bony human lead us to the long boardroom where the pack leaders convened. The room stretched endlessly before us, and the most powerful people in my world sat at a shiny oak table. I felt like we'd interrupted a conference in session rather than appeared for a requested meeting. I choked back a nervous laugh—like this could be called something as civil as a *meeting*. A flurry of moments centered around one man, and he read through a sheaf of papers without looking at us.

Alain smirked from where he stood behind our leader, our Alpha. The large man's dark hair was lightly peppered with grey. Jerrod and I bowed our heads before him in respect.

"You know why you've been called before us." Malcon's deep voice carried down the table.

Jerrod took a half step forward. "Yes, and I would dispute the validity of the claim against us."

The whole room drew a breath, and I concentrated on keeping my face expressionless. Well, my mate wasn't pulling his punches this morning. I hoped like hell that he was playing this situation right, but I trusted him to get us through this. The way I didn't yet trust Lena. And that was what our problem boiled down to. I had faith that Jerrod could confront our leaders and win, but I didn't know Lena well enough to have that same faith.

Everything had happened so fast, and that instantaneous connection of the soul hadn't meant my mind was keeping pace. We needed that chance...to develop the potential into something strong. A trust as unbreakable as the mate bond between us. I took a breath and let those realizations settle. Yes. That was right. Whether we stayed here in L.A. or needed to move somewhere else, the most important thing was our mating. Jerrod understood that, and so did Lena. It had just taken me a bit longer to catch up.

I knew I craved stability, something my mother had never provided after my father died. She'd flitted from one wolf to the next, always looking for that mated connection, but she never found it again. And I never knew who I was coming home to—a quiet, competent mother who made sure I had what I needed or her neglect while she focused on keeping the man in her bed happy. Jerrod had given me that stability, and Lena, through no fault of her own, might strip it away from me. But what she brought was something more precious. Something my mother craved more than anything. A mate. A connection. Belonging. I had been so stupid, so blind. So damn scared.

I would fix this somehow, but for the moment, I needed to help my other mate get us out of this mess. I forced myself to focus on the people in the silent boardroom.

Malcon finally glanced up, pinned us with his gaze. "You *dispute* the concerns of your pack leaders?"

My mate didn't back down, his chin angled stubbornly. "I have the highest respect for my leaders, sir. *However*, this claim calls into question the instincts of my mates and me. How can that possibly be valid? No one can dictate what instincts we receive."

"Your instincts seem fallible with your stance on werewolf-vampire relations at your place of business." Alain's slick voice cut across anything the other men might have said.

Jerrod glared coolly, a direct challenge in his gaze. "You're confusing politics with instincts, Alain. The two have nothing to do with each other. Try to remember that. And it's not my politics that are being called into question." His gaze locked on Malcon. "Is it?"

The older man steepled his fingers together and pressed them to his lips. When he spoke, it was slowly, the words considered. "No. No, it's not."

"Sir, you can't possibly—"

"Be silent, Alain. This is not your concern." Malcon didn't deign to turn and look at him. "And do not ever tell me what I can or can't possibly do. Is that clear?"

The man's eyes bugged out of their sockets, and he turned a very nasty shade of purple. He choked out, "Yes. Sir."

I barely hid a grin, focusing on the middle button of Malcon's dress shirt so Alain couldn't see the mockery I knew would flash in my gaze. He was a greasy little prick, and this might be the first time he'd ever been put in his place. He'd danced to the leader's tune his whole life, and it had gotten him where he was. The Alpha's right hand. I wondered how long that would last now. More changes for everyone. Malcon didn't seem much like his father. Interesting times lay ahead for our kind...at least in L.A.

"I swear, as does my mate Rachel, that Lena is our mate as well." Jerrod ignored Alain to focus on the Alpha. "We have mated in the tradition of all werewolves. How can that be refuted?"

Malcon nodded before he focused on me. My spine straightened, and I forced my eyes to meet his. It felt unnatural, disrespectful, but I didn't let myself look away. I swallowed and lifted my chin.

A small grin quirked the side of his mouth. "What of you, Rachel? Do you stand behind your mate?"

"Beside them, sir. Both of them." I pushed my hair over my shoulder and tried not to fidget nervously.

He hummed in the back of his throat. "Alain tells me your other mate, Lena, left rather abruptly this morning."

"Not everything with a new mating goes smoothly, sir." I'd never made a truer statement in my entire life. A wry smile pulled at my lips.

An answering grin formed at the side of his mouth, and I noticed for the first time that he was a handsome man. "So I've seen, but I've never experienced it myself."

"I'm certain you will, sir."

At that, he let loose a short bark of laughter. "Any pointers for my future bride?"

I considered the question more closely than maybe I would have normally. My own recent mating wasn't going all that well. And my actions affected not only Lena and my relationship, but

Jerrod and Lena's, and Jerrod's and mine. A delicate balance, and I better learn to walk that tightrope fast. For all our sakes. "The only advice I have, sir, is: Hold on tight no matter how scary it is. Mating is as much a test as it is a joy."

"I'll keep that in mind should I ever find her." His grin slid away as he sobered abruptly. He faced my mate. "As for your politics, Jerrod." He tilted his head. "I would say you're very fortunate that this didn't happen two months ago. I'm a bit more...open...to peaceful relations between our people and the vampires than my father was."

Jerrod nodded. "Yes, sir."

A murmur broke out down the table, and Malcon silenced it with a single glance. So, he was using us as a way to make a political statement on his rule. Okay, then. As long as it worked out well for us, I was totally on board. The Alpha took a breath. "Times are changing. Vampires and werewolves are no longer a secret to humans. We must make strides to find a lasting peace between our people, or we'll die. How long do you think humans would let us conduct open war before they interfered? We might be stronger, older, but they still outnumber us. I'll have no interference. I'll have no more war.

"Anyone in the pack who disagrees may leave with my blessing. Anyone who remains and tries to gainsay me...will regret it before they die." He focused on my mate again. "Times are changing. One of those changes may be that a man might have two mates at once. I am not one to question the instincts of a wolf. They are not ruled over by law—mine or any other Alpha's. Especially when that wolf's instincts have always been commendable in *all* areas."

"Thank you." Jerrod's chin dipped in a respectful nod.

The Alpha returned the gesture. "Bring your mate before me tomorrow. I'll speak with her and see if she would make a good member to our pack."

"Yes, sir. And she will, sir."

"That's all for today."

Jerrod opened his mouth to speak, and I latched my hand over his forearm and leaned toward him. "Let's get while the getting is good."

"Hell, yeah." He glanced down at me, nodded, wrapped his fingers around mine and drew me out of the room.

When we exited the building, the cool of the late fall afternoon wrapped around me, and I realized sweat had stuck my shirt to my back. My breath rushed out with relief, and I stopped to brace my hands on my knees. "Holy shit."

Jerrod's hand rested warm and comforting between my shoulder blades. "Well. Malcon seems nice enough."

I laughed, angling a glance up at him. "You're insane, you know that, right?"

"It's part of my charm." His fingers cupped my elbow and drew me upright. "Come on. We dodged one bullet, but we have another problem to deal with."

A sigh eased past my lips. "*I* have another problem to deal with. You didn't do anything wrong."

"Yeah, well. We're in this together, Rach." He shrugged. "Not everyone is going to agree with our new Alpha, and we can't force them to...so let's deal with what we *can* fix."

Chapter Six

It took Jerrod the rest of the day to track Lena's scent to an apartment building in North Hollywood. Which was a good thing because I sucked at tracking. But once I got inside the building, her scent drew me like a Lorelei to her apartment. I took a deep breath, and I could smell her in there. This was definitely the place. Lifting my shaking hand, I made myself knock firmly. I'd messed this up. I would have to mend it.

"Go away." She probably hadn't spoken above a normal volume, but my werewolf hearing picked up her words.

Leaning my forehead against the smooth wood, I gripped each side of the doorjamb in my hands. "I'm not going away, Lena. Please open up."

Silence greeted me. Tears welled in my eyes. I'd hurt her. I knew it. So tough and stubborn on the outside, but vulnerable to me...and Jerrod. And I'd betrayed that with my fear and anger. "Please, my mate. Don't deny me."

The door snapped open, and I swayed as its support fell away from me. My hands tightened on the jamb. Rage sparked in Lena's dark eyes. "Deny you? The way you denied me?"

All the words I'd mean to say, all the apologies I'd practiced in my head slid away. I scrambled for something—*anything*—to say. "We spoke to the pack. You need to go before the Alpha tomorrow, but from what he said, I'm pretty sure they're going to accept you as a member."

"And that makes everything okay?" She swung the door to shut it in my face. "Goodbye, Rachel."

I caught the door in my hand, each of us applying a bit of our superhuman strength. It stayed half-open, neither of us strong enough to overpower the other. "No, it doesn't make it all right. I just wanted you to know."

She glanced over my shoulder into the hallway. "Where's Jerrod?"

"Downstairs." A weak smile curved my lips. "He's giving me ten minutes to get my foot out of my mouth before he comes up."

"Why bother?" Bleakness entered her eyes, and she relaxed her grip on the doorknob. "I know where his loyalties lie."

My hand snapped around her wrist. She tensed, a shudder running through her. "With us. His loyalty is to both of us. Could you really ask him to choose? He's mated to us both."

She shook her head until her ebony curls whipped around her shoulders. "I know who he would choose."

"I don't."

"What?" Shock flashed across her face. Good, I had her attention. Now if I could just make her listen to me, forgive me for being a royal bitch.

I shook her arm lightly. "Why do you think it would be so easy for him? He needs us both."

"But the two of you—"

"Were incomplete without you. As much as I love Jerrod— and I do more than anything—he can't fulfill all my needs. I want men and women. It's always been that way for me. Always. But when Jerrod came along, I thought that was it.

Game over. Fate had decided I was going to be straight for the rest of my life, and things were so good between us that I accepted that—Jerrod, too. We didn't have any secrets, so he knew what I gave up to mate with him." A wicked grin teased the corners of my mouth. "He did everything in his considerable power to make it worth my while.

"Then...then you showed up, and it terrified me to think that fate was going to give me everything I ever wanted, but it might come at the price of everything I'd ever worked for. I was scared that we'd lose our home, and I didn't stop to think that you weren't as attached to it as we were. I also didn't stop to think that a home isn't the most important thing. Yeah, it would suck to have to leave everything, but losing my mates would be worse than losing any material thing. I was cruel, and I was wrong." I swallowed back tears. "I hurt you."

"Yes."

I nodded, met her gaze with the all the open honesty I could muster. No shields, no more room for doubts and fears. "I'm sorry, Lena."

She stared at me for long moments, tension running through her body. She sighed and closed her eyes, sagging a little. "Don't do it again."

"I won't." I offered up a wry smile. "I'll probably make other mistakes, but not that one."

"Everyone makes mistakes." Her lips pressed together, and she looked away. Stepping back, she let me inside. She turned and led the way to a big couch upholstered in black leather. Her arms crossed tight over her ample breasts while she propped herself against the arm of the couch.

I reached out and cupped her cheek, running my thumb over her silky dark chocolate skin. Leaning forward, I rested my forehead against hers. "I'm sorry, my mate."

"Rachel." Her full lips brushed against mine when they moved, and I didn't bother to fight the shudder that ran through me. My eyes slid shut. God, the feel of her, the smell of her. I wanted her, but I savored the warmth of her lush body pressed against mine. This was precious. This was what was important. My mate. Both of my mates. I wasn't foolish enough to think this was the only hurdle we'd have to get over before we managed to balance the complexities of a three-way mating, but it was worth it. This feeling, this peace that wrapped around me. This wholeness, like the halves of my sexuality, of my soul, had finally come together. For so long, I'd been denied this side of myself, and I needed to embrace it.

Her mouth whispered over mine again, and heat shot through me, pulsing through my sex. She slipped her hand into my hair, twining her fingers through the length of it. Tugging on the dark strands, she angled my chin up so she could kiss me. Her tongue flicked out. "I've missed this. Not even a day and I crave it like an addict."

"That's how it is between mates."

She sighed against my lips. "I don't know if I'll ever get used to it."

"You will. Jerrod and I will help you." I pulled back a little to look at her. She was so lovely.

"Are you sure that you can handle this? I don't—I couldn't stand it if I made you unhappy." Her dark eyes shimmered with tears, but she coughed and blinked them back, glancing away.

I cupped her jaw in my palm and pulled her around to face me. "I have issues with change. You didn't do anything wrong. I want you. I want to be mated to you. Jerrod and I went before the pack leaders to make them see we belong together. Forever. You're ours now."

She nodded. "I can only trust that you mean it."

"I do. You can tell me to pipe down if I say anything like that again. That's Jerrod's favorite approach. That and fucking my brains out until I forget about what I was freaking about. I prefer that approach, frankly."

A small huff of laughter erupted from her throat. "I'll keep that in mind."

"Good." I cupped her hips in my hands and slipped down until I knelt before her. "In the meantime, I think I should really make this up to you somehow."

Her eyes widened, and she sucked in a breath that lifted her breasts. I wanted my lips on them, wanted to suck them deep into my mouth and bite her nipples. "Wh-what did you have in mind?"

"Can't you guess?" My fingers hooked in the waistband of her yoga pants. She lifted her hips from the couch so I could ease them down her legs.

"Show me." She grinned, her teeth flashing white against her cocoa skin.

She wore nothing under her pants. No underwear. Well, my mate wasn't shy. Come to think of it, neither of them was. Then again, I wasn't wearing panties either. We were well-suited, the three of us. I smiled against her skin as I moved forward to kiss the slope of her belly. Her breath caught when I moved lower.

Slipping my hand between her silky soft thighs, I tugged one of them up to rest over my shoulder. She was wide open, and I could see how slick she was for me. Juices glistened on her pussy lips. I glanced up to meet her gaze. A moment of sheer heat and anticipation spun between us. My heart raced so fast I could hear it pounding in my ears. "I'm going to make you scream for me, Lena."

A naughty little grin lit her face. "You can try."

I licked my lips, letting my gaze fall to her sex. The musky scent of her filled my nose. I slipped my fingers up her thigh to rub over her wet folds. She moaned and arched her hips a little to open herself further for my touch. A gasp strangled out of her when I plunged two fingers deep inside her, beginning a fast pace. She fell back on her hands, clutching the leather of the sofa arm tight. Her hips lifted into my thrusting movements. I leaned forward to press my lips to her sex. The flavor of her burst over my tongue as I licked her clitoris.

Cream pooled in my sex, slipping down my legs. The taste of her turned me on so much, I could almost come right now. I closed my eyes and shuddered. My nipples peaked tight, thrust against the front of my silk shirt. The prim calf-length skirt I'd worn to meet with the pack leaders rode up to bunch around my thighs as my knees slid apart on the slick tile floor. Cool air brushed over my pussy, contrasting with the heat rushing through me.

"That is the hottest thing I have ever seen." The rough edge of Jerrod's voice caressed my ears. When had he arrived? I'd been so focused on Lena, I forgot he was following me up, forgot we hadn't locked the door behind us. I heard the bolt slide home and the heavy tread of Jerrod's boots as he walked toward us.

"Hello, Jerrod." Lena's tone was Sunday morning casual. Grinning against her slick flesh, I nipped her clitoris hard. She squealed, her fingers twisting in my hair to the point of pain. I winced as fire spread down my scalp, but somehow it was more of a turn on than anything else. The muscles of her thighs quivered against my shoulder where I held her open.

Jarrod kneeled on the couch behind her, sliding her shirt over her head. His palms covered her large breasts, tweaking her dark nipples. She moaned while he bent her over the arm of the sofa to suck the tight crests deep into his mouth. I knew from experience how his teeth would nip and his tongue would sooth the erotic sting.

Her body twisted when I chuckled against her damp flesh. I suckled her hard little clit while I worked my fingers deep inside her. She writhed in my arms. Her walls clenched around my fingers, and I could tell she was going to come. I angled one finger to rub over her G-spot and she screamed, a long, high, keening sound. Her pussy milked my hand while Jerrod grazed his teeth over her tight nipples. She sobbed, her body shaking as she collapsed in our arms.

Jerrod tugged her onto his lap and cuddled her close while I climbed onto the couch with them. She reached out an arm to pull me in, and we curled together, nothing but the sound of her soft sobs cutting the silence. My heart clenched with each one, knowing whatever pain she felt was my doing. I took a breath. I wouldn't hurt her like that again...but the love that made people vulnerable was what broke their hearts, so there was no guarantee I wouldn't hurt her again *at all.* I could try, though. And I would. Her breathing quieted to soft hiccups while I rubbed her naked back.

She sniffled, wiped her eyes, and leaned back in Jerrod's lap. "You're hard."

He coughed, a flush of passion racing under his skin. She rolled her hips against him, making him shudder. His fingers bit into her soft flesh to hold her still, and his eyes glittered with hard passion. "I said watching the two of you was the hottest thing I've ever laid eyes on. I wasn't kidding."

"I have an idea." Her eyebrows arched, and that wicked look I was beginning to associate with her returned to her eyes. She scooted off his lap and stood. Jerrod and I followed her lead, and he reached out to pull my back to his front. I could feel the rigid heat of his cock pressed to my bottom. Lena's gaze went over my shoulder to look at him, a little smile crossing her face. Oh shit. This did not bode well for me. Molten heat rushed through my body. God, I knew how creative Jerrod could be, I couldn't imagine what he would do with help.

He leaned me forward, his big palms cupping my ass. His hands gathered my skirt up until it was around my waist, and then he slid his fingers in until they spread my cheeks wide. I shuddered, pressing back into his touch. He dipped in further to swirl around my anus, and further still to push inside my ass. He withdrew to move to my pussy where he gathered my wetness and trailed it back to my anus. Again and again until his fingers slid easily in and out of my ass. My muscles shook with need. I wanted more. Anything and everything he could give me. "Please."

"I'm going to please you. Don't I always?" He stretched me wide, sliding two and then three fingers into me.

"Yes." I shuddered at the impact as he thrust in and out, each push faster and harder than the last. Desperation clawed at me, fierce and insatiable. "More. Please, more." He pulled his hand away, and I moaned aloud. I arched my back to try and keep his thrusting digits inside me. "No. I need more. Please."

The head of his thick cock nudged against my ass, pushing steadily in until he was seated to the hilt within me. The stretch bordered on pain, but I didn't care, I needed to quench the fire that burned through my veins. It consumed me, made me rock my hips towards him even as I sobbed for breath. He grasped my hips, holding me still, and I choked on the need to move. The muscles in my body tensed as I tried to wriggle in his grasp. Lena cupped my breasts in her palms, moving her hands down my body as she knelt before me. Oh God. Want exploded hot wild inside me.

"Let's make it interesting. You need to try new things and change a bit...to learn *balance*, right, Rach?" One of her fingers slipped between my legs, dipping inside my pussy. One finger, two, then the hard ball of her fist. I whimpered at the stretched sensation. I hadn't been fisted since my last female lover—years before I'd mated to Jerrod—and I'd almost forgotten how much I'd always liked it. How I reveled in the feel of each knuckle caressing my inner flesh, how it made me whimper, but I was so wet it made the slide possible. How it was almost too painful to bear, but the ecstasy was so worth it. That it was Lena's hand inside me, my mate, made it so much better than it ever had been before. Jerrod nudged in deep so that they were both inside me at once. I was so full, so taken by them. Reality slid away into nothing but the feeling my mates pulled from me. They set a slow, maddening pace for me. First Lena's hand would fill me, then Jerrod's long, hard cock. Over and over and over until I wanted to scream.

"*Yes.*" My hips rocked back and forth as their rhythm picked up speed. Balance, just as Lena had said. I was caught between them, balanced on the razor's edge of pleasure and pain, only able to follow their lead toward the promise of ecstasy. God help me.

I reached one hand back to clench on Jerrod's thigh and the other forward to twine in Lena's thick curls. They anchored me in the wild storm that ripped through my system. My entire body was more alive than it ever had been before, every inch of me tingling, shaking with the sensations I couldn't control. They controlled them, controlled me. And I trusted them both to take me where I needed to go. With that I let go of everything but my need. Heat boiled inside me, consuming me. I closed my eyes and rested my head back on Jerrod's shoulder, tears leaking down my cheeks as I twisted my hips to move with them. His tongue flicked over my collarbone, over his mate mark. I choked, my sex clenching hard. His hand rose to cup my breasts and pinch my nipples, rolling the tight tips. Lena's fingers moved to stroke me just so, and a scream tore from my throat as I came.

My pussy fisted around Lena's plunging hand while she worked me harder and faster, pushing me higher than I'd ever gone before. She leaned in and bit the inside of my thigh, sinking her fangs into my flesh. I jolted in shock, shuddering over the edge into orgasm again. Jerrod slammed deep once more and froze, his come pumping into my ass. He groaned low in his throat, the sexy sound echoing in my ear. It was too much, too fast. Blackness swam through my vision, and I swayed on my feet. One moment I was shivering in the aftereffects of orgasm and the next the world went dark as I fainted.

When I resurfaced I was alone in an unfamiliar bed, but before I could panic, the mattress dipped as my mates crawled in on either side of me. Lena curled against me on my right, her leg looping over my thigh. I scooted so that my head pillowed on Jerrod's arm, and he idly toyed with my nipples. Slow desire coiled through me, and I knew we'd soon be rolling together on the wide bed. For now it was just us and the quiet that surrounded us. For the first time in my life, I felt whole. Replete. All the pieces of my soul were in place. Jerrod and Lena fulfilled me.

His hand slipped down to circle my belly button. Tears filled my eyes as Lena reached out to twine her fingers with his on my stomach. Emotion flooded my heart, made my breath hitch with the sweet intensity of it. I laid my palm over their hands. The three of us—joined until death. A grin tugged at my lips. Contentment ballooned inside me. "I love you, my mate. Both of you."

I wasn't naïve enough to think that Malcon's approval would make everyone in the werewolf community accept us, but I would fight tooth and claw for my mating. Of that much I was certain. It was that simple and that complicated. Jerrod was right. I couldn't force the world to agree with us. Not that I'd ever admit to a *male* out loud that he was right. It just wasn't seemly. I could only work to strengthen our bonds. The rest we would solve later. Together. For now, I had them in my arms, and I would make the most of every second we had. With any luck it might be another fifteen decades before we parted.

A huge smile spread across my face. I'd been right. It had been one hell of an anniversary. And I was glad the three of us shared it.

Big Girls Don't Die

Dedication

For Desi, who made the sweet suite inspiration for this story possible. For Eden Bradley, who picked up her phone just when I needed her and is an excellent shoulder to cry on when you're stranded on the shoulder of the road. For Emily and Nicole, who invented the uterine homing device. For crazy nights, crazier tow truck drivers, truth that's stranger than fiction and falling down the rabbit hole.

Chapter One

That damn evil hellcat.

I was in the shower just as my day began, right at the crack of sunset, when a huge crash sounded through my teensy bathroom. I jerked back the curtain to see what the hell was going on, when Beelzebub streaked across the floor and tackled the overflowing trashcan, which spewed the contents everywhere. And still, he attacked the trash. *Shit.* A cold rush of dread made my stomach do back flips. Somehow, I *knew* he'd cornered a rodent. In my bathroom. With me trapped, sopping wet and stark-ass naked in the bathtub. This was a hell of a way to start Valentine's Day.

So. I had to deal with the whole mouse situation, not the least of which because he was about to slaughter the thing on my landlord's cream-colored carpet. And who carpets a rental in cream? I hopped out of the tub and into the scattered trash. Wads of things I didn't even want to think about were stuck to the bottoms of my wet feet.

Since I couldn't kill it, I had to get rid of it. What did I do to deserve this? I caught sight of myself in the floor to ceiling mirror and tried to ignore the fact that all I could see reflected back at me were my wide blue eyes. What I couldn't see was the rest of me, the pale skin, the mile long legs and too-generous hips and thighs. The dripping black hair that was sleeked to my scalp. The pointy fangs. None of it, because I was a walking spawn of Satan.

I tossed Beelzebub into the living room, grabbed the tallest glass from my kitchen and played tag with the stupid mouse until I finally scooped it up and slammed a plastic dish over the top. No need to let it try and escape, right? Right.

Then I realized I was still buck-naked, and I had to toss the mouse out into the yard. After I set the glass on my dresser, I snatched my nightshirt off the dirty clothes pile and pulled it over my head. With my Winnie-the-Pooh nighty stuck to my wet skin and the mouse in a glass, I jerked the door open and launched my uninvited guest...right into the broad, scrumptious chest of my worst nightmare.

Andre St. James, the man responsible for turning me into the undead. His large dark-skinned hand snapped out and caught the tail of the mouse. When he brought it up to his eye level, the hairy little guy squeaked in mad terror, prey before a predator. I could relate. I'd had those pale celery-green eyes trained on me enough times to know that I melted into an orgasmic puddle within a few seconds. He dropped the mouse that, like a smart little rodent, ran like hell. Unlike me, who stayed where I was with my mouth agape.

"Cynthiana." The way he said my name, with an emphasis on the first syllable, made it sound like something naughty and sinful. His *Noo Awlins* accent made everything sound naughty. The man could read a phonebook, and I'd get turned on.

Heat flooded my body, and my nipples tightened. His gaze zoomed right in on the pointed tips. I swallowed.

Don't panic, girl! He's a bad, bad man who turned you without asking pretty please first. Even if he was gorgeous and had skin like yummy milk chocolate. Even though he tasted just as good as he looked. Delicious in every possible way.

Mmm-hmm. Wait, what was I thinking? Bad, bad man. Remember? *Shit.*

"Yes, Satan?" I propped my forearm on the doorjamb and cocked a hip. My other hand kept a death grip on the doorknob. Right now, it was the only thing keeping me from flinging myself at him and begging him to shake me all night long.

His full lips quirked, and I swayed toward him. "Invite me in."

"No." The word escaped as a sigh.

His long finger lifted to stroke my elbow, the only part of me that stuck out of the doorway. Hot flashes rippled out from the touch, and I wanted to rip my nighty off and run around with my panties on my head. If I had any on. Which I didn't.

"Invite me to come inside."

"Come inside *me.*" The words fell out of my mouth before I knew what I meant to say. Warmth rushed up my cheeks. *Oh, shit on a stick.* I had not just said that. I *had not.*

"As you wish, *cherie.*" A full-blown smile spread over his face. Damn, it made his already gorgeous features just...perfect. My stomach executed a slow flip. He stepped over the threshold and shut the front door behind him.

I put up a hand and scrambled back. "Wait. Wait, wait, *wait.* That's not what I meant."

"I've always considered you a woman of your word." He kept coming toward me. Stalked me. One step forward for him and two steps back for me. I couldn't let him touch me again. The night would start out with a bang. Literally. That would be a huge mistake. I'd done that before and look where it got me. One-way ticket to Fangville.

My back hit the door to the bedroom. His green eyes promised wicked pleasure, and I already knew he could deliver. Heat flashed through me, and I pressed my thighs together. My breath panted out. Wetness flooded my core. *God help me.* I squeezed my eyes closed, but I could smell him. His musky scent mixed with his expensive cologne and curled into my nose. It intoxicated. I've never wanted anyone the way I want him. It just wasn't fair. Why him? Why the undead?

"Don't come near me."

He ignored me. Each second brought him closer and closer until his heat enfolded me. With each of his hands braced on the doorframe, he penned me in. "How am I to come inside you then, *cherie?*"

My head tilted back, my throat exposed. His gaze caressed my neck, my breasts and my hard nipples. The clingy wetness of my nightgown cupped my sex and thighs. Want twisted through me, my muscles tight with anticipation. Possessive, he looked at all of me. I should have been pissed that he'd barge in on my life after months of staying away. Even if I'd told him in no uncertain terms to do so. When he'd turned me, he'd ripped my life apart. I didn't have to play nice about it. But all I felt right now was the need to be sexed hard. And *that* pissed me off.

"Why the hell are you here anyway?"

"I'm here for you." Simple. Bald. And so freaking wrong.

"I don't want—"

"Don't you?" His gaze flicked to the less than subtle jut of my nipples again.

Damn it. Totally betrayed by my own horny body. My muscles shrieked for me to arch into his chest, press myself to him. He was right there. I wanted to touch him, wanted him to touch me. Stroke me. Fuck me.

No. I bitch-slapped my hormones into submission. To play with this man was dangerous—

He dipped his head to graze my neck with his soft lips. I shivered at the contact of his skin on mine, all thought fizzling away. My eyes half-closed as erotic memories flashed in my mind. Memories of us together. My head tipped to the side, and I gave him full access to my neck. Because I wanted. Damn the man. Oh, wait. He was damned already.

The doorknob rattled as he twisted it, and the solid surface behind me disappeared. I fell back, but his arms snapped around me, and I was plastered against his chest. *Yes.* Even the thin cloth of my nighty was too much to separate my skin from his. Naked. That was the ticket.

I bucked against him, the urge to be closer too strong. "Andre, I need..."

"*Oui, cherie.*" His hands cupped my ass, lifted me against him, and I wrapped my legs tight around his waist. The hard length of his erection rubbed between my legs as he carried me toward the bed. Every step sent sensations screaming through me, as his hips ground against mine. My empty sex clenched hard. God, I wanted him inside me.

We fell back against the mattress. His heavy weight spread me wide. He thrust against my naked pussy. The fabric of his slacks added friction to the movement. Tingles raced down my arms and legs. Lust burned in my belly. He rotated his hips, his hard cock grinding against my clit. *Oh God. Oh God.*

"Andre!"

"Cynthiana." He breathed my name like a prayer as he pulled back to look at me. Peeling the bottom of my still-damp nighty up, he stripped me in less than a second and left me bare to his gaze. I shivered and dug my heels into the backs of his thighs.

"Hurry."

"Say please."

One of his hands slipped between us. His knuckles brushed my pussy as he worked at his fly. I lifted my hips to keep the contact. He chuckled, his zipper rasped, and his fingers lingered to stroke my slippery skin.

With a press of my fingers against his smooth scalp, I pulled him down to caress his lips with mine. I coaxed him with my tongue as it slid along his bottom lip. I suckled it and nipped the skin with my teeth hard enough to draw blood when I pulled away. "*Please.*"

His jaw tilted, and I could see the arteries pulse beneath the skin. I licked him, a gentle slide of my tongue down the length of his neck. The muscles corded, and his blood called to me. Need, longing and bloodlust twisted inside me until I couldn't tell one from the next. My fangs ached at just the thought of feeding. Yes. Now. I bit him and felt the sweetness of his lifeblood flow over my tongue. As if he'd been waiting for my bite, he thrust his cock into me so deep that he slammed against my cervix. I came hard, and my pussy fisted, repeatedly milking him.

I braced my hands on his shoulders, threw my head back and rode out my orgasm. His hands gripped my hips while he worked me on his cock.

He bent to suck my nipple into his mouth, then flicked his tongue over the hard tip. "*Tu es belle. Je t'aime. Je pense tout le temps a toi. Mon coeur.*"

I loved when he spoke French to me, even though I understood nothing he said. The words, the accent, the heat of passion in his voice. It made me burn hotter. My nails dug into his shoulders. His fangs slid into my skin as his cock buried in my pussy over and over. I was pierced in every way.

He froze for a long moment before his hips rammed into mine once more. Shuddering, he flooded me as he orgasmed. He ground himself against my pussy, stimulating my clit.

"Andre!" I screamed his name as I came again. It went on and on forever. My whole body throbbed. He sank his fangs deeper into my flesh, and my eyes rolled back in my head as I fainted from the overwhelming sensations that slammed into me.

When I woke up snuggled against him with my cheek pressed to his broad chest, my eyes almost popped out of their sockets. I jerked upright and wrapped the sheet tight around my breasts.

His hand settled between my shoulder blades, and I jerked away. "Why are you here?"

He cleared his throat. "It's Valentine's Day."

"So?" I flicked a glance over my shoulder.

A grin tugged at his lips. "It is a day to celebrate lovers. I wanted to celebrate with you."

"We aren't lovers."

"I beg to differ."

"You can beg all you want, but we're people who have fucked twice, not lovers. This isn't love."

"Cynthiana—"

"Don't say my name. Just don't say anything. Please go."

"What?" His voice went soft, dangerous.

"Go. Leave. I know you speak English." Yeah, so I sounded like a raging bitch. He hadn't done anything I hadn't asked for, but now I wanted him to leave. That should be a move he had down pat.

I hauled myself to the edge of the bed and stomped into the bathroom. I would take my shower, and he could take himself off. Maybe I could wash that guy right out of my hair and try not to dwell on the fact that I was a moron who slept with him *again*.

Brushing a hand over the embroidered ice blue silk of my very short dress, I made sure everything was presentable. It was my own design, like everything else I wore. I used to model. *Plus-sized models exist, I swear.* So if anyone could show off my clothes to their greatest advantage, I could. If I won't wear my products, why would anyone else? I'd busted my ass for years, but my career as a clothing designer had finally begun to turn enough profit that I could quit modeling over a year ago. Not that I'd ever be rich. I just didn't have to work two or three jobs anymore. Good thing too. The whole can't-see-myself-in-the-mirror or on film issue would be something of a career killer for a model.

I stepped through the door of Eclipse, the most notorious club for things that went bump in the night. Smart humans didn't come near the place. But I wasn't human anymore. Thanks to a certain annoying, sexy, rude, great in bed, undead vampire bastard who shall not be named. Damn it.

My best friend Candy and I planned to meet up for an anti-Valentine's Day drinkathon tonight. Neither of us had a love interest—Andre so, *so* did not count—so, we intended to see how long it took before one of us worshipped the porcelain god. I would bet she out drank me and I did the psychedelic yawn way before her. She'd probably stand behind me in the bathroom and pretend to be supportive, while subtly mocking me for being ten feet taller than her and a total lightweight. We had a well-refined relationship at this point.

The door swung open behind me, and a rush of cool night air slid over my skin. "Hey, babe."

I turned to see Candy enter. The lupine grace of the werewolf race made her look taller than she was. She looked good in my designs, too, when she didn't have on Gucci or Prada. And her Dior purse made me drool.

"Hey, hot mama."

As a vampire, I wasn't supposed to be friends with her, but fuck that. Candy was my girl. I didn't give a flying rat's ass whether werewolves and vampires hated each other's guts. So there. The wicked-nasty fighting between our two races forced every kind of magical creature—fairies, demons, witches—out of the closet about ten years ago, and the world hadn't been the same since. Of course, the new werewolf Alpha in L.A. had made some major changes in vampire-werewolf relations recently, so I'm guessing Candy got way less flak for hanging out with me than she used to. I'd never been hassled much, and I'm not sure if it was because I'd metaphorically flipped all vampires off or because Andre had stepped in and stopped them. I didn't like to think Andre had ever done anything I should be grateful for, so I shut down that line of thinking and followed Candy across the crowded room. She nodded to her acquaintances as we approached the bar. I only recognized a few of the people present.

Jerrod, the werewolf bartender, flashed an easy grin. "Cyn and Candy. My two favorite flavors."

I snorted. "Whatever."

"Blow me." Candy propped both hands on her ample hips.

Jerrod leered at Candy's cleavage. "What'll you have?"

"Jack Daniels. A double, please." She rolled her eyes. While Jerrod liked to flirt with the customers, he was happily mated to *two* women. He and his mates had made some waves in the werewolf community by having more than one mate at once. That was a new thing for the hairy ones, apparently.

I cleared my throat. "I'll have a strawberry margarita."

Candy turned to me. "Uck. How can you drink that fruity shit for wimps?"

"Sticks and stones."

"How old are you? Five?"

"Compared to you, yeah. Old hag." Candy just had her thirtieth birthday, and since I was still twenty-nine I took every opportunity to rub in her over the hill status. It was what I got in exchange for my inability to hold my liquor. At least she wasn't as old as Andre. He was turned way back in the 1850s.

Hey, I did go out on one date with him, and stayed for a one-night stand that became the undead nightmare. Sucking a girl's blood without asking is such a party foul.

Candy's mouth opened to blast me with a snarky comment when her gaze flicked over my shoulder and her eyes widened. "Incoming."

Andre. Had to be. Why did he have to be here tonight? "Oh, fuck me sideways."

"I'm sure he already did." A knowing grin pulled up the corners of her mouth.

"How—"

She tapped the side of her nose. "I can smell him on you. Want me to kill him for you?"

Okay, for half a second I was tempted. Candy might be short and curvaceous, but she was feisty as hell, and could probably take on both of us without much effort. His big hand closed around my bare shoulder, and I shivered. Not because I was cold, but because just having him this close made me horny. Wet. Turned me into a raging, ready-to-have-sex-in-a-public-bathroom kind of slut.

"Excuse us for a moment, Candace." His fingers slid down to cup my elbow.

She arched a brow. "Do anything she doesn't want and I'll make you cry for your mommy."

"I've never been one to deny a woman her pleasure, but I'm occupied at the moment."

I widened my eyes at Candy and all but popped them out of their sockets in an attempt to communicate that she should not, under any circumstances, leave me alone with him. She smirked. Her expression said plainly that I could put my big girl panties on and deal with my own damn problems. *Bitch.*

Candy disappeared from sight as Andre drew me into the swirling crowd. Somehow he slipped us through the crush of bodies and into a secluded corner by a side exit. His green eyes reflected in the low lighting. His hand bracketed my chin and tightened when I jerked back. Irritation flashed through me, and I glared at him as he forced me to meet his gaze.

His lips flattened into a line, his face serious. Emotion I couldn't read shone in his eyes. "I knew we were destined for each other the moment I saw you."

I sighed, suddenly tired. "I didn't."

"That doesn't mean it isn't true. I was just ahead of you in realizing it."

I shook my head and tried really hard to get a grip on my bitchiness. It wouldn't help to go off on him again. "Maybe you should have waited for me to catch up."

Now it was his turn to sigh. "Cynthiana, try to understand. I have been alive for many, many years. In that time, I have had more than my share of women—enough to know the moment I saw you that you were mine. Forever. If I hadn't bitten you that night, I would have *literally* spent eternity kicking myself if, for example, you'd been hit by a car and died the next day. I couldn't risk waiting for you to catch up. Humans are so fragile. I had to know there was some safety for you, some small guarantee that you wouldn't be snatched away by fate."

Right, like I was letting the safety argument fly. *So* not buying it—that it was all for my best interest. I poked him in the chest. Hard. "You didn't even *ask*, Andre. That's a big ass decision to make without me, the woman you're *destined* to be with. If that's how you like your relationships, I'm not interested."

A look that was almost...hurt...crossed his face. My heart squeezed just to see it, but I stomped my tender emotions into submission. I was denying him his new favorite toy. Me. And I was no man's toy.

My cell phone trilled in my handbag. *Oh shit, what now?* I fished it out. The bottom dropped out of my stomach as if I were on a rollercoaster. The number for my co-dependent hooker of an Aunt Misty flashed on the screen. An honest-to-God prostitute. No kidding. When she called, it was never good news. She wanted money, or she was in trouble, or *both*. If it wasn't for my ten-year-old cousin, Desi, I wouldn't talk to her. She was self-destructive poison. I mean, no one grew up and said, "I want to be a crack whore someday."

Ignoring the disgruntled look on Andre's face, I turned my back on him and put the phone to my ear. "Hello?"

"Cyn! Oh, thank you, God! Desiree was in a car crash and broke her leg and has a concussion, and you know I don't have insurance and—"

A cold, hard knot settled in my belly. God, no. Not Desi. "I'll be there as soon as I can."

I hadn't even gotten my drink.

Chapter Two

My hands clenched on the steering wheel. I had to get to my cousin. That's all I could think. Please, please let Desi be okay. I loved that little girl so much. I was going crazy right now. Worry gnawed at me like a hungry werewolf. One quick look at the speedometer told me that I was about ten miles over the speed limit. They wouldn't pull me over for that, would they? I pushed my convertible Mini Cooper a little faster.

Flicking a glance down while I punched the speed-dial, I tried to get Misty on the phone for a progress report on Desi. It was a few hours to Las Vegas from Los Angeles, but if I hurried I could be inside the hospital before dawn. Something else to get pissed at Andre for. No reflection, no sunlight.

My stomach rumbled. Oh, yeah. Cravings for blood. Another lovely side effect. When was the last time I had fed? I meant to have something substantial before I went to Eclipse, but Andre had sort of interrupted that plan. I'd barely taken any blood from him, so my stomach felt as if it was digesting itself right now.

"Hi, this is Misty and Desiree, leave us a message—"

"Damn it." I huffed out a breath and tossed my cell phone on the passenger seat.

My gaze swept the barren landscape along I-15. There wasn't anything for as far as I could see except dirt and stars and a few ragged Joshua trees. When I glanced back at the road, a large white jackrabbit hopped in front of my car.

"*Shit.*" I jerked the wheel and swerved to miss it, but the crunch of bone sounded as it bounced against the underside of my car. "Oh, that is just nasty."

And then my tire blew up. Rubber popped. The Mini Cooper's back end spun out. My heart stuttered as my pretty little car made grinding noises when the metal of my tire rim hit pavement.

"Shit, piss, motherfucker. Oh God. Oh God."

Skidding off onto the soft shoulder of the road, the car finally came to a stop. I sat there and panted while my heart rate galloped. My knuckles showed white on the wheel, and I had to force myself to relax my grip and reach down to shift into park. My hands shook on the door handle when I hauled myself out to go look at my tire. I walked around the car to the passenger side and kept an eye out for crazy-ass drivers who might be too blind or stupid to see the emergency flashers on my car and hit me. Oh, yeah. That was the flattest tire I'd ever seen. Little bits of rubber hung off it and flopped on the ground.

"Spare tire, Cyn. Put it on and get the hell to Vegas." Popping my trunk, I—*What the hell?*—Where were the jack and tire iron? I had forgotten to check for them in this car when I bought it from the used car dealership last week. Now that I needed 'em, they were nowhere to be found. Fan-damn-tastic. Time to call in reinforcements.

I opened the passenger door and fished around for my cell phone. Please, please, please let me have cell phone service. I was in the middle of bumfuck nowhere. I squeezed my eyes shut for a moment, not daring to look. My breath whooshed out when I saw I had full bars. I pulled in a deep breath while I dialed my roadside assistance number. The number was programmed into my phone, just in case. You never knew when a Rambo-wannabe jackrabbit would hang on to your bumper and use his last breath to shred your tire. Fucking bunny.

I punched in all the appropriate numbers and listened to a recorded voice tell me to call 911 if it was a life threatening emergency. Well, duh. "Hello? I have a flat tire, and I need someone to come put on my spare—"

The woman dispatcher's professionally concerned voice cut me off. "Okay, ma'am. Are you in a safe area?"

I looked around at the miles and miles of dirt. "I'm kind of in the middle of nowhere, but I guess I'm safe."

"Good. Now where are you exactly?"

"I'm not sure. I'm eastbound on I-15 about a hundred miles west of Las Vegas. I don't see a call box or any mile markers."

"So, you're east of Las Vegas—"

"No, I'm *west* of Vegas going east *toward* Vegas." I rolled my eyes.

"What city did you just pass?"

Did I just speak English? I swear I'd told this woman I had no idea where I was. I was worried about Desi, not about where I might pop a tire. "I'm not sure. I know I'm about a hundred miles west of Vegas."

"All right, ma'am. We'll dispatch someone, and they should be there in about twenty to thirty minutes."

"Thank you!" I could be with Desi soon, then. I shivered as the cold desert night air hit my bare shoulders and legs. Hurrying back to the driver's side, I slid into my seat.

Twenty minutes later, my phone rang. Oh, good. Must be the tow truck driver.

"Hello?"

An older female voice responded, "Hi, Ms. Trent. I'm sorry, but we won't be able to dispatch anyone until we know your location. Can you tell me exactly where you are?"

I blinked. "Um. I already told the last lady I talked to."

"Can you tell me again?"

Okay, stay calm. I'd only been on the side of the road for about half an hour. Everything was fine. "Sure. I'm not one hundred percent sure of where I am, but I'm eastbound on I-15 about a hundred miles west of Las Vegas."

"Are there any mile makers nearby?"

"No." And I sure as hell wouldn't wander around in the frigid ass desert to look for one.

She was silent for a long moment. "Um. All right, ma'am. We'll dispatch someone, and they should be there in about twenty to thirty minutes."

"Sounds good." I sighed and dropped the phone on my lap.

Twenty minutes later, my phone rang.

"Hello?"

A pleasant male voice answered. "Hi, Ms. Trent. I'm sorry, but we won't be able to dispatch anyone until we know your location. Can you tell me exactly where you are?"

My head was about to explode. I spoke slowly and carefully, as if he was a small child. A stupid small child. "No. I. Don't. Know. Where. I. Am. I told the last two people that I'm a hundred miles west of Las Vegas on I-15. That's the best I can do."

"I'll have to put you on hold for a moment to see if I can't get the tow truck company to three-way this call so you can tell them."

What could I possibly tell them? *I don't know* was pretty easy to relay. "Okay."

Music pumped through the phone, followed by a discussion of how I wanted the company's homeowner's insurance in case my house blew up, burned down or shook to the ground in a mega earthquake. The first time it was funny. After thirty minutes of listening to it on a loop, I was suicidal.

Tears pressed hard against my eyelids. It was dark, and I was all alone out here. Not a single car had passed in the whole time I'd been on this call. The night closed in on me, cold and suffocating. All I could hear was the damn elevator music and my harsh breathing as I tried not to cry.

"Ms. Trent?"

"Y-yes?" I sniffled and covered it with a cough.

"I'm sorry for the wait."

I cleared my throat. "No problem."

"Are you sure you can't give us more specifics on where you are?"

"No, I really can't." My tone was flat. Just shoot me now. My stomach rumbled. I really, really needed to feed. Soon. I took a moment to think about how I would drain this obnoxious bastard dry if he were here.

"My wife always knows where we are on round trips, so I thought you might too."

So now my geography was linked to my gender? Because I was a chick, I automatically knew my exact location? *Yeah, whatever. Your wife just rocks my world. Tell her to come find me then.* I bit back the words that wanted to rip into this guy and damn near sank a fang through my tongue. It wasn't his fault I had a flat tire. I counted to ten in my head. Backward. The screaming need to get to Desi just wouldn't quit. She needed me, and I was stuck in the middle of the Mojave Desert.

"All right, ma'am. We'll dispatch someone, and they should be there in about twenty to thirty minutes."

I sighed. "You know, that's what the last two people said as well. I kind of have my doubts at this point."

"We're doing our very best, ma'am."

"Right. Okay. Twenty to thirty minutes." I hung up.

Twenty minutes later, my phone rang. Oh, that was just *it*. I was so changing to a different roadside service when I got home. This was just ridiculous.

I stabbed the answer button and tucked the phone under my chin. "What?"

There was a long pause. "Cynthiana?"

A familiar voice. Relief rushed through me. I didn't even care that it was Andre. It was *someone* I knew. I clutched the phone tight to my ear.

"Andre." My voice broke on his name.

"Are you all right? Where are you?"

"*I don't know.*" I just lost it and sobbed hard into the cell phone. I'd never get to Desi tonight, and the sun would come up, and I would be scorched to death. The end.

"Shh, *cherie*." His tone soothed. "Tell me what happened. Perhaps I can help."

I covered my eyes with my hand. "You c-can't. No o-one can. I'm all alone."

"I'll come to you, and you won't be alone."

"I told you I don't *know* where I am." Fat tears slid down my cheeks, and I just knew my mascara had turned me into a vampiric raccoon.

"You don't need to know. I'll find you. Where did you intend to drive?"

My breath hitched. "I w-wanted to go to Las Vegas on I-15. My cousin got hurt."

He hummed sympathetically. "Then you should get there soon. What happened?"

See? *See?* Someone understood how important it was to get there *now.* And that someone was Andre of all people, but right now I was okay with that. I told him the whole thing from the second I ran out the side door of Eclipse to the last operator who called me.

My voice rose with frustration and indignation when I told Andre about the guy's wife comment. "I almost screamed at him. 'Wait, let me consult the GPS reading from my uterine homing device. I forgot to turn it on until you asked *for the third time.* The beacon's up now, man. You should be able to see me from space.'"

His low, rich chuckle sounded in my ear. Hot warmth tingled through my body. God, just the sound of him turned me on. I pressed my thighs together and set my hand against my belly in an attempt to quell the gathering need.

Think about something else, quickly! "And how many white jackrabbits are there? It doesn't matter, because there's one less now."

"I'm certain the rabbit deserved his fate."

I grinned for the first time in hours. "Yeah. Evil bunny. And it popped my tire."

"Bastard."

"Yeah. *Yeah.*"

He laughed again.

A thought struck me. "Why did you call me anyway?" He didn't answer, and I thought I'd lost signal or my battery died.

"Hello?"

He spoke slowly. "You ran out and I was...concerned."

"Really?" The thought warmed me. It shouldn't have, but it did. The more time I spent with him, the more I liked him. He was addictive, and I'd turned into as big a crack whore as Misty.

"*Oui, cherie.* I'll come to you as soon as possible."

I opened my mouth to speak when headlights pulled up right on my bumper. "Wait. That's okay. The tow truck driver is here. And...thanks Andre."

"Don't get out of your car!"

My hand froze on the door handle. "Why?"

"Make certain this is the person you called for. There are those who would take advantage of a woman alone."

"Andre—"

"Please?"

I blinked. I don't think I'd ever heard that word come out of his mouth. Ever. It rattled me. "O-okay."

Feeling like a fool, I sat there and waited for the tow truck driver to come fetch me.

"Do you have anywhere to stay for the day?" Concern laced Andre's voice.

"I'm staying with my aunt."

"Her home is light-proofed?"

"I'll be fine, Andre."

"I know the owner of The Creole Resort and Casino. Tell the front desk that you're my guest, and they'll give you a comp room."

"Andre—"

"I get rooms there for free any time I'm in Las Vegas. I'll call ahead so it's available if you'd like, and dinner is also complimentary. No pressure. I hope your cousin is well."

"I...thank you." He wouldn't try and force me? Coerce or coax? This was the guy who turned me on the first date? Had I actually managed to get through to him? My eyebrows winged up, and I snorted. *Nah. Not Andre. He probably had gas or something.*

A loud knock on my window made me jump. Right. The tow truck driver. "I have to go."

"Be careful, *cherie*."

"I will."

"Swear it?"

"Promise. Goodbye." I flipped the phone closed and opened the door. The frigid desert air closed around me. I shuddered in the cold. I wished I had a jacket. Or a snowsuit. Goose bumps erupted down my arms and legs, and my nipples got rock hard. I crossed my arms over my chest when the driver's eyes zoomed in on them in the dim light from my car's interior.

He grinned from beneath his long, messy beard. "How long you been stuck here?"

My teeth clattered so hard I was about to crack a fang. "A long time. I have a flat tire and really need to have my spare put on so I can get to Vegas, but I don't have a jack."

"A flat? Dispatch told me you broke down. I got nothing to change a tire."

My eye twitched. "What?"

"I don't have anything to change a flat."

Breathe, Cyn. Breathe. "You're a tow truck driver, and you can't change a tire?"

"Nope. I can tow you to Vegas though. You got the extended roadside service, right?"

"Right." My teeth ground, and I bared my fangs in a nasty smile.

The man paled and stepped back. "Ah. Let's get you loaded up then. Why don't you sit in the cab of my truck?"

"Fine." I bent and snagged my bag and phone from the car. I just know he stared at my ass while I did it.

My heels sank into the loose dirt as I limped over to the truck and grabbed the door to haul myself up. I snapped the seatbelt in place, and my phone rang yet again. It better not be my roadside people, or I would give them a piece of my mind. Misty's number flashed on the screen.

Thank the sweet baby Jesus. She could tell me what was going on. "Hello?"

"Cyn?"

My heart lurched, and I squeezed the phone so tight I thought the plastic might crack for a second. "Desi! Are you okay? What happened?"

A drama-queen sigh sounded through the connection. "Mom *totally* exaggerated. My friend's mom had a fender bender. No biggie."

"She said you had a concussion." Desi was okay? My brain wouldn't quite wrap itself around the idea.

"Nah. I got a lump on my head."

"And a broken leg." My heart started to settle into a normal rhythm. Oh, thank you, God. Thank you, *God.*

"That was the *other* guy. He was on a motorcycle. Sucks for him, huh? Anyway, um, I'll stay at my friend's house tonight, so you don't need to come. Sorry Mom freaked."

I deflated a little. "Oh. Well, I'll come by tomorrow since I'm almost there."

Her sweet little girl laugh made me smile. "You are? Yay! I'll see you in the morning."

"It'll have to be after dark, hon."

"Oh yeah. Oopsy. Bloodsucker babe."

I laughed as relief made me lightheaded. "Okay, sweetie. See you soon."

"I love you, Cyn. Like, a ton."

"I love you too." My heart felt too full just then. I adored that kid. Too bad she had to grow up with Misty. She was a great kid now, but what would happen when she grew up and figured out how her mom brought home the bacon? If she didn't already know. A sad sigh slipped out.

The driver's door opened, and my scruffy chauffeur hopped in. "Where to, ma'am?"

"Um. The Creole, please." If my options were a hotel room or spending Valentine's Day alone with my aunt, I'd so take the hotel room. This was the least romantic Valentine's Day ever, and I would much rather be tossing back a whole lot of booze with Candy at Eclipse.

The truck shuddered as the driver shifted into gear. I glanced back to see if my car was secured. He better not fuck up my Mini Cooper. I'd waited for over a decade to afford a nice car. We pulled onto the freeway at about five miles an hour. This would be a long ride.

"You know what the worst part of this job is?" My driver grinned companionably.

Do I want to know? Not really. My night pretty much sucked ass at this point, so of course I got the tow truck driver who wanted to lay his problems on me. Super.

He started to talk about all of the motor vehicle accidents he'd ever pulled someone out of. Mostly teenagers. All of the people he knew and went to school with, his kids knew and went to school with. Right. I so wanted to hear about this when I'd spent the evening thinking Desi might lay broken in a hospital room from a head-on collision. I cringed when he went off on semi-trucks and what they do to convertibles with liquored up kids in them. *It would be rude to clamp my hands over my ears, right?*

Could this night blow any harder? I squelched the thought. No need to tempt fate by asking the no-no question, even inside my own head. My stomach growled again. Hunger ripped into me. I closed my eyes and tried to focus on something else. I could smell the driver's blood, and I wanted it. My tongue rolled around my parched mouth. I was desperate for distraction.

"We're here."

My eyes snapped open. The wild orgy of neon lights down the Strip assaulted me. I loved Vegas. It was so unapologetic about what it was, a city of sinful indulgence. It was loud, brash and tacky. It said money with an edge of sleaze. I sighed as a tight smile pulled at my mouth. My fangs rubbed against my lips. Made it before dawn. Now I just had to find somewhere to feed.

I collected my things as the driver backed my car into an empty space in The Creole's parking lot. This was the newest and most expensive hotel on the Strip. It had the architecture and scrolled wrought iron that screamed New Orleans. No wonder Andre liked this place. Beautiful fountains out front spouted water in time to classical music. The driver shook my hand before I turned to walk toward the hotel. I felt the veins pulse beneath his skin. My ears buzzed from the hunger. I dropped his hand like a poisonous snake and jerked away.

Every step was weaker—my legs shook beneath me. Icy tendrils slipped down my spine. The massive glass doors slid open to admit me, and the crazed lights of the slot machines blurred before my eyes. I swayed a bit before I managed to walk through the big white marble lobby. Ironwork surrounded the front desk, and flickering lanterns hung suspended over the staff member standing there. The black counter gleamed in the low light.

"Hello... I'd like to check in." I braced my hands on the desk to steady myself.

He took one look at me and stepped away from the desk. Great, he would call security because I shook like an addict. When the world spun, I closed my eyes to make it settle.

"Ma'am?"

"Yes?" The man stood before me and held out a tall glass of red liquid. Blood. I snatched it from him and downed it like a shot, chugging the cold tangy nectar.

His half-smile flashed a long fang. "You looked a little pale."

I set the glass on the shiny counter. "Thanks."

"Your name please?" His hands hovered over his computer keyboard.

"Cynthiana Trent. I'm a guest of Andre St. James."

Every inch of the skinny man froze for a moment before he resumed his movements. His voice squeaked a bit. "Of course, Ms. Trent. Here's your key. Let us know if you need anything, anything at all."

"Oookay." He just got all weird. What was that about? I shook my head. Never mind. People got strange around Andre. I guess even his name could do it. Rubbing my shoulders to ease the long night of tension, I tried not to wince. God, I was tired.

The walk back through the casino was a trip. A million reflective surfaces showed nothing but a pair of floating blue eyeballs. I couldn't wait until I'd been a vampire long enough to start seeing my reflection again. Unfortunately, it could take a hundred years or more.

Of *course*, there were a million banks of elevators, and they all went to different sets of floors. I was way too tired for this many options. How tall was this building anyway? I had no idea, and at this point I really didn't care enough to investigate. Stepping into an elevator that should go to my floor, I poked the right button. The door slid closed, but nothing happened. My brow wrinkled as I stared at the panel. *Oh, do not let me get stuck in this damn elevator.* That would so top off this crappy night. I pressed the button again, harder this time, just in case it was a funky button. Still nada. Zilch. Zip. *Nien.* Denied.

"Shit."

Then I saw the tiny sign that read "Please insert keycard here" with a little slot to do just that. Oh. Duh. Heat rushed up my cheeks, and I was grateful no one was here to see this. This was a weird hotel. I'd never had to use my key to make an elevator car move before, but maybe it was some new security thing. I shoved my keycard into the opening and pressed the button to my floor.

The elevator rose smoothly upward. I leaned against the cool glass wall while exhaustion weighed down my body. A bed sounded great. Hotel rooms were all the same, but I'd give kinky sexual favors for a shower and mattress right now. Too bad Andre wasn't here. I snorted in self-disgust. What could I do about his "destined for each other" stance? The man was too stubborn to give up, but what did I want? I just didn't know. He was so sweet and so damn pushy at the same time.

I sighed, too tired to think about this. The elevator slid to a stop, and the doors opened to let me out.

"Whoa." I jerked to a stop. This wasn't a hallway lined with doors. This was a foyer with one set of double doors. Oh. Shit. This was the *penthouse.* When Andre said a comp room, he meant the fucking penthouse. Shock rolled through my system. My hand shook as I lifted the key to the slot recessed into a gold panel beside the doors. Maybe it was a mistake. But no, the fancy curved knobs clicked. I reached out and twisted, and the doors opened on silent hinges.

A huge breath escaped my lungs as my heels sank into the deep carpet. The whole room was done in an explorer theme. A huge globe was set into a polished wood table in one of three seating areas. I had my own kitchen and bar. There was a bathroom and *two* televisions, one of them a big screen. There was a dining room big enough for twelve. Why would anyone have twelve people in a hotel room? Behind the table was a wall of windows that overlooked the Strip. Lights twinkled for miles before they gave way to the inky black of the desert.

"Ooooh." Now that was a view.

I stepped around the entertainment center and through the door I assumed led to the bedroom. My eyes bugged out.

"Wow," I breathed.

The same floor-to-ceiling windows continued in here, and right next to the windows was a massive black hot tub. Four people could fit in there easily. Two plush robes were folded and stacked on top of the wide shelf that surrounded the tub. On the opposite side of the room stood an enormous four-poster bed. I chuckled. Four people could fit in there too.

My shoes clicked on the marble floor in the bathroom beyond the bed. I had to explore the whole suite now. There was a shower with tons of nozzles that would spray me from about ten different directions. This place was crazy. Still-just-barely-making-the-bills girls like me weren't allowed in rooms like this unless it was to clean up after people like...Andre. I sighed, then almost fell out of my cute shoes when the phone beside the *toilet* rang. Wow, they could take a dump and do business at the same time. That was real multitasking.

Reaching out a tentative hand, I picked up the receiver. "Hello?"

"Hello, Ms. Trent. What may I get you for dinner? Or perhaps a cocktail? Compliments of the hotel owner, of course."

Right. Andre said it was all on the house. My stomach growled like a rabid, frothy mouthed werewolf. Though not for blood this time, thank goodness. Free food sounded too good to pass up just now. "Um. Can I order something to eat?"

"Of course, Ms. Trent. What would you like?"

Something simple. Something that wouldn't freak me out. Something I could afford without breaking open the piggy bank. Which was probably nothing on their menu. "A chicken salad sandwich, please."

"Of course. What would you like to drink? We have every blood type on tap."

"O negative, please." I drank the same blood type that I had. It made it more bearable for me, as if I just got some kind of daily transfusion. *That made sense, right?* Less "bloodsucking undead whore of Satan" and more "poor chick who got a vampiric STD out of the one-night stand from hell".

"And would you like that in a glass or shall I send up a sheep?"

Sheep, the vampire term for humans. Maybe it made them feel better about sucking them dry, but it all still seemed a bit twisted to me. "In a glass. Thanks."

"We'll send a bellman up shortly."

"Okay."

Some people would think I should be used to this, but modeling wasn't the glamorous work Hollywood made it out to be. Hours spent frozen in muscle-straining, back-breaking positions where the photographer went ballistic if you breathed too deeply and messed up his reference points and lighting. I got to wear the forty thousand dollar necklace for a photo shoot, but it wasn't mine. None of it was for me. But this was. All mine. For tonight anyway. A giddy laugh bubbled out, and I danced in a little circle.

I plopped onto the bed and fished some cash out of my purse to tip the bellhop. Eyeing the huge hot tub, I promised myself a swim as soon as I finished dinner.

A sharp knock sounded from the living room. "Room service."

I heard the door open as I walked out of the bedroom. A tiny woman in a tuxedo set a tray with covered dishes on the bar. She took a few bottles off the tray and stooped behind the counter. "Ahem."

She straightened, a strained smile on her face. Her words tripped over themselves. "Ms. Trent. I just wanted to stock the mini-fridge with O negative i-in case you get thirsty later. Compliments of the owner."

What was up with these people? Did Andre terrify them so much that they were scared of me by association? Or, wait. Did I look like road kill? Like the rabbit I squished into a bunny pancake? That would scare anyone. I couldn't even see myself in a mirror to check. Ack!

Lifting the covers off my dinner, she revealed the most enormous chicken salad sandwich I'd ever seen. With golden crispy French fries piled beside it. My mouth watered as the aroma curled toward me.

I smiled at the bellhop, but she shuddered and stepped back. Ah. A human who had a healthy fear of vampire fangs. Smart. Unusually smart. I wondered if she ever pulled sheep duty. Probably not. There were humans who liked the job. Some even got off on it in a super icky way. I tossed the tip on the bar, grabbed the tray of food and walked backward toward the dining room.

"Thank you. Have a nice night."

Crystal Jordan

"Of course, Ms. Trent. Please let us know if you have any other needs." She scooped up the cash and darted for the door.

Chapter Three

Floating naked in the hot tub, I let the swirling water tug at my hair. The heated jets loosened my knotted muscles. A contented sigh slipped out. I didn't even want to consider how bad this night would have ended without Andre. A night with Aunt Misty just couldn't compare to a penthouse suite. The mere thought of Andre made the hot water feel like a caress against my skin. I wished it were his hands that moved over me. My nipples tightened, and my pussy clenched on emptiness. Fire flooded my system as I shuddered.

I jerked upright, ripped from my little fantasy when a knock sounded on the door. Water coursed down my face. I swiped it out of my eyes and tucked myself next to the side of the tub to use as cover.

The same woman's voice called out. "Room service."

I frowned. "You already—"

"A bottle of champagne, compliments of the owner." I heard the front door slam as she left.

I wasn't even surprised when Andre entered the bedroom cradling two flutes of bubbly. A grin pulled at my lips, and I was...happy to see him. That was a surprise. A definite change from the start of this hellacious night.

He toasted me with one of the glasses and handed me the other. "Compliments of the hotel owner."

I took a sip, and the bubbles tickled my tongue and lips. "Uh huh. And who might the owner of this hotel be?"

"Me."

"You just happen to *know* the owner, huh?"

"Intimately." A look of worry crossed his face, and fine tension ran through his body. I noticed he hadn't had any of his drink. "Are you all right? You were treated well?"

"Your entire staff is terrified to fuck up in front of me." I leaned back a little to look at him as he walked closer.

A dark smile crossed his face. "They should be."

"Why?"

He settled on the ledge that wrapped around the hot tub. "Because you're my...friend. I expect my friends to be treated very well."

Friends. I'd never thought of him that way, but it didn't feel wrong. It fit. Friends with benefits fit even better. His muscled thigh was less than an inch from me, and his scent enticed me. He needed to be naked. My gaze ran up from his leg to the bulge of a large erection pressing against the expensive fabric of his slacks, over the wide expanse of his chest to the light green fire in his eyes. I took a deep breath, which lifted my breasts from the water and made it lap at the beaded tips. His gaze dipped to skim my naked body, and I damn near whimpered.

"May I join you, *cherie*?" His deep voice rumbled the request.

What the hell? Let's face it. This tub had been made to have sex in. I met his gaze and licked my lips slowly. "Yes."

His breathing hitched. He reached forward to run his fingers through my wet hair and cupped my jaw in his big hand. I leaned into his touch, my eyes never leaving his. He stood and watched me watch him as he undressed. Oh, now, this was a show not to be missed. I moved back to the end of the tub, propped my arms on the edge, and waited.

A slow smile pulled at his full lips, and his lids slid to half-mast. His jacket hit the floor while his nimble fingers loosened his silk tie. He flicked open the buttons of his shirt to reveal the smooth skin of his muscled chest. Thank you, God. I could watch him forever. He was such a gorgeous man. I *could* watch, but I'd rather participate.

"Now the belt." I would explode if he didn't get in the tub soon. The movement of the water stimulated *everything.*

His fingers tugged at the buckle to leave it hanging while he fumbled with his fly. "You enjoy this?"

"Hell, yes. Hurry up, or I'll start by myself in here."

He paused in his undressing. Damn it. "That would be...interesting to see."

"More interesting than doing it yourself?" I cupped my hands around my breasts, lifted them and tweaked the nipples.

"*Mon Dieu.*" He groaned and shoved his slacks to the floor, then toed off his shoes before he strode toward the tub. As he stepped over the ledge, I met him halfway. Our lips touched, and our tongues stroked together. His arms tightened around me, pressing me to his chest. I moaned into his mouth when his cock jutted against my belly. He lowered us into the swirling water, and it caressed us, sealed us together.

My head fell back. "Please, Andre. I can't wait."

I gasped as he lifted me to set me on the lip of the tub. Teetering, I leaned back to grab the outside edge of the shelf that surrounded the hot tub. He shoved my thighs wide and pulled my knees over his shoulders. His wicked grin flashed up at me before he licked a path up my thigh. Heat exploded through me, and I panted.

He switched to the other leg and offered it the same treatment. His hot, wet tongue against my skin was amazing. Goose bumps erupted down my arms.

"Don't stop," I begged. He was almost where I needed him.

His lips parted on my thigh, and fangs sank into the corded muscle there. He drank from me. Licking, sucking, stroking with his tongue and teeth. I came so hard starbursts flashed before my eyes. My pussy spasmed, and a tingle of heat raced through me.

I threw my head back. "*Andre.*"

My hips arched hard as I tried to press closer. His tongue swirled down between my legs as his lips closed around my clit before he sucked hard on the nub. I screamed, and my hands slipped on the ledge. He caught me before I fell, pulled me back into the water, and held me to his chest as I panted in fear and quivered with passion while my heart ricocheted in my chest.

He pulled my thighs to straddle his lap and rubbed the tip of his cock against my pussy. I tightened my legs around his waist to seat myself on his dick. My breath hissed out. He was so big, the stretch almost hurt. But, man, it hurt so good.

His legs flexed as he pumped into me. He went slow, teased me, and tortured me. I sank my fangs deep into his neck. His big body shook as his hips slammed into mine. I sucked at his throat and flicked my tongue against the sensitive flesh.

"Cynthiana! *Je t'aime. Je t'adore*, Cynthiana." His voice was harsh in my ear.

I released his neck to lick out to his shoulder. "Come for me, Andre."

My fangs bit into the muscles of his broad shoulder. He groaned long and loud as he froze against me, then he pounded forward. One, two, three short, hard strokes and he came inside me. He kept moving, kept pumping into me. I jolted when his lips touched my shoulder, kissed, licked, and then his fangs sank into my skin. Lust slammed into me as fire licked at my core. I lifted my knees to press my heels against the small of his back. His hands slid between us to toy with my clit, and I sobbed as I came again. Hard. My pussy milked him, fisted tight over and over. Still he moved, pushing me higher. We shuddered, sank our fangs deeper, drank from each other, cherished each other. Loved.

Then my eyes rolled back, and the world went black. The last thing I felt was Andre's arms as he cradled me to his chest.

"Why can't I drive my own car?" I folded my arms over my chest as I slumped against the leather upholstery of his limo. The car pulled away from the front of The Creole to maneuver through the crush of cars in the large circular driveway and down the Strip. Aunt Misty lived on the edge of town.

"Because the mechanic still has to replace the tire."

"I could have done that myself." *As soon as I got my hands on a jack and tire iron.* But I suspected that he'd instructed the mechanic to take his time so I'd have to spend the evening with him.

This limo would look great as it pulled up in the trailer park. I dropped my head back against the seat and closed my eyes. Shit, I didn't want him to see my scary aunt.

"You are being unreasonable."

Maybe, but no way in hell would I admit it to him. Last night had shaken me. Somehow I'd let the man past my defenses, and now I had to deal with how to keep him from taking over my whole world. Somehow.

"You can pay for it yourself, if it pleases you. I won't apologize for making a phone call while you slept. I also called and had one of my servants go feed Beelzebub."

God, I was such a horrible cat-mommy. I hadn't even thought about Beelzebub since I got the call from Misty. But *Andre* had thought of my pet. I opened one eye to look at him. "You'll let me pay for something?"

He shrugged. "If it's what you want. I do have a gift for you, though."

"More than this?" I swept a hand down my outfit. I'd found it beside the bed when I woke up. I'm a designer. I know exactly how much these clothes cost, and I squirmed in discomfort.

Reaching into his breast pocket, he pulled out a long slim box and handed it to me. I flipped open the lid.

"Oooooh." An illusion chain held a suspended cluster of sapphires. The jewels gleamed against a bed of white satin. My fingers hesitated before I let them stroke over the stones. I shouldn't touch it. It was too much. It was sparkly and shiny, and I wanted it. *Mine, mine, mine.*

I pulled back. "Andre—"

"It's a gift."

"I can't."

"I can. It's a gift." His gaze held mine steady, and I knew this was important to him. Why, I wasn't sure, but I couldn't say no.

Disappointment flashed in his eyes when I handed the box back to him. "It's beautiful. Will you help me put it on?"

He blinked for a moment before a blinding smile spread over his face. Yeah, so this was a win for him. I turned my back to him so he wouldn't see my own grin. He slipped the necklace around my neck, the metal cool against my skin. He dropped a kiss to the side of my neck. "Compliments of the owner."

I froze as shock twisted through me. This, *this* was why I had so much trouble dealing with him. The possessive, *I'm always right* attitude. "I don't have an owner."

His hands closed over my shoulders to spin me around. "Cynthiana, look at me. I'm half-black. You know when I was born. My father was also my *master*. If anyone knows that slavery is wrong, it's me."

"And still, you make decisions for me. As if I don't have the mental capacity to make the right choice for myself. As if you owned me. Would you like a list of examples?" I shoved his hands away.

The look on his face was priceless. It was half pissed-off man and half bitch-slapped, naughty little boy.

He winced and glanced away. "You're right. I...have no excuses."

"Okay." Did he actually apologize? That was what it sounded like, and I must be insane.

"I'm sorry, *cherie*. For all of it." He sat back against the seat and turned to look out the window as the lights of the Strip gave way to the streetlamps of residential neighborhoods.

I shifted, uncomfortable with the awkward silence. Time to change the subject. "How—how long have you been in the hotel business?"

"About a century. I bought my first in France. My father sent me there after I was turned."

"Why hotels?"

He shrugged. "An opportunity presented itself, and I took it. I was better at it than I could ever have imagined. *C'est la vie.*"

"How many do you own?" Okay, so I was curious about how a man like Andre became...well, a man like Andre. This stuff doesn't come up on the first date.

"I have The Creole in Vegas, one in Atlantic City, and a third in the works for Monte Carlo. The rest are resorts in the Caribbean, Europe and Australia."

"I see." Wow. I knew he was wealthy, but...damn. The necklace shifted against my skin as I took a deep breath. I laid a hand over the chain.

He cleared his throat. "What happened to your cousin?"

I grinned. Looked as if I wasn't the only one who needed a subject change. "She was in a car accident. She's fine. Her mother overreacted."

"Mothers can do that. Is she all right then?"

I nodded. "I just want to see her before I leave. Since I'm in town."

"You're close to her? How old is she?"

The grin spread wider over my face. "Desiree—Desi is ten going on forty. She's a great kid."

My smile slid away as I thought of the life she had to grow up in. God, it just sucked.

"What's wrong, *cherie*?"

Reality burned me, and it hurt to even admit this. I tried not to think about it, ever. "I—Before you turned me, her mom wanted to let me adopt her. But...well...not now. Because I'm a vampire."

"Her mother is irresponsible?"

To put it mildly. "Yes."

He sighed and squeezed his eyes shut. "Then I have more to apologize for than I knew. This is why you were so angry with me? Not just turning you, but what my actions denied you?"

"That sums it up nicely, yeah."

Pain flashed in his gaze, and he spread his hands. "It doesn't help, but I am truly sorry."

Shrugging, I looked down at my lap. The anger at him slid away. Yes, he was pushy. Yes, I had a right to be angry. But in the end Misty being Misty wasn't his fault. "How could you know?"

"I hurt you." His voice was tortured.

I reached out and grabbed his hand. "Andre..." But what could I say? It wasn't all right. Not for Desi, not for any of us. "I forgive you."

His fingers closed around mine, and I saw a million questions run through his eyes. His thumb ran down my palm and made me shiver with a need that wouldn't quit.

"How bad is it for your cousin? Bad enough that the state may take her away? Could you get custody then?" Those questions from him weren't what I expected.

"Please. What judge in his right mind would give a human child to a vampire? They think we all suck." I pasted a look of feigned surprise on my face. "Oh, wait. Guess what? They're right."

He snorted. "I can try to help."

"No. Please. I think I should ask Michael to help."

"Your brother?"

"Yeah, he's a lawyer. He'll know what to do."

I could almost hear his jaw grind that I would ask someone before him. He released a deep breath and lifted his fingers to slide them through my hair. "Whatever you think is best."

Holy shit. Blow me over with a sneeze here. "Who are you, and what have you done with my Andre?"

"I *trust* you to make the right decision."

My mouth flapped open, but nothing came out. My chest tightened at his words. *Whoa.*

His lips pursed, which just brought his fangs into view. "I *can* change. I have a choice in this, *n'est pas*? I want you that much."

Still I just sat there while my heart pounded. *Say something, Cyn! Say anything!*

He hummed in the back of his throat. "*Your* Andre. I'm glad to see you catching up, *cherie.*"

I slapped his chest, laughing. "You are so—"

Dipping forward to kiss me, he cut off what I intended to say. Not that I minded because, right now, I couldn't really remember anything but how good his lips felt on mine. He licked his way into my mouth, and I bit his tongue lightly. The kiss heated as we fought for control of it, became desperate as I panted against his lips.

His fingers lifted to stroke across my cheek, and some sweet emotion I couldn't name spun inside me. Damn, but I craved this man more than my next breath. The thought would have freaked me out yesterday, but at the moment it just felt...right. A shiver went through me. I didn't want to examine my feelings too closely, so I distracted myself. With Andre.

Reaching between his thighs, I slid my fingernail up the inside seam of his slacks until I could cup my hand around his cock through the fabric. His groan vibrated against my lips. Breaking the kiss, he threw his head back against the seat. "Cynthiana, I..."

"Yes, Andre?" My voice came out a low purr, and I let an evil grin curl my lips. I unfastened his belt and slid down his zipper, dipping my hand into his pants. My fingers curled around the hot velvet of his hard flesh, pulling his dick free. Rotating my palm over the head of his cock had him locking his jaw and gritting out a low groan.

He swallowed and for the first time ever I watched the big vampire struggle for coherency. Power flooded my veins, and heat throbbed in its wake. I loved that I could do this to him. I doubted many could, and the thought made my smile widen. My sex was so hot and wet, I was going to scream if he didn't touch me soon. His hand covered mine, guiding my hand up and down the long shaft. "How long do we have until we reach your aunt's home?"

"Ten minutes." I glanced out the window to see where we were. "Maybe fifteen."

"I'll take it." His fingers bit into my hips as he hauled me onto his lap, parting my legs so I straddled his muscular thighs. He jerked my skirt up to my waist. Though he'd thought to get me new clothing for today, he'd forgotten underwear. His fingertips stroked deep between my legs, honing in on my clit. Then again, maybe he hadn't *forgotten* anything. Bracing my hands on his broad shoulders, I closed my eyes and rolled my hips to increase the stimulation. "Andre, hurry. I want you inside me. Right *now.*"

"Anything for you." He pulled his hand away and replaced it with his cock. He nudged at my entrance, but I wasn't willing to have any kind of delay. Now meant *now.* Relaxing the muscles in my legs, I enveloped him in one downward push.

Goose bumps shivered over my flesh, and I arched into him. He lifted his pelvis to meet me halfway. Our movements were harsh, urgent. I couldn't get enough of him. I needed this connection—even if I struggled to deny any other connection I might have with him. Our lungs bellowed, a harsh rasp of sound in the quiet interior of the limo. He filled me over and over again, faster and faster.

"More." My voice erupted, a rough demand, every part of me screaming for the satisfaction only he had ever given me. "*Andre.*"

"*Oui,*" he groaned, his palms cupping my ass as he worked me harder. "*Je t'aime.*"

He moved a hand inward until he could swirl a finger around my anus, and I froze with his cock buried deep inside me, shuddering when he pressed into my ass. Shock made my breath catch. A little smile kicked up the corner of his full lips. He rubbed his finger against the head of his cock through the thin wall that separated the two. I bit back a scream. Jesus Christ, no one had ever done something like this to me. It was fucking amazing. My hips bucked, moving myself on his thrusting cock, his long finger. I moaned when he added another digit, stretching me. Heat rocketed through my body, and I sobbed for air. Oh, my God. Oh. My. God.

Clenching my inner muscles around his hard cock, I made him groan. "*Merde*, Cynthiana."

My fingers tightened on his shoulders, and my pussy tightened on his dick. Spasms built in waves, pleasure thrumming through me with every movement. I skated on the very edge of ecstasy with each stroke of his cock, each thrust of his fingers into my ass. A low scream ripped from my throat, and my hips twisted. "I'm going to...going to..."

"Come," he ordered, and I obeyed. I had to. I couldn't stop myself. My head fell back as my pussy fisted on his long dick. Orgasm dragged me under until I knew I was going to die. He arched beneath me, slamming his cock inside me again and again until he froze. His come jetted into me, filling me.

His green eyes softened as he looked at me, something tender and worshipful in their depths. He held me close as I came apart in his arms. Tears slid down my cheeks as that same sweet emotion wrenched inside me.

Never let it end. That was all I could think. Please, God. Never, ever let this end.

Chapter Four

"Cyn!" Misty slurred my name so that it sounded like *shin*. She stumbled off the rotted, saggy plywood porch that stood outside her crappy trailer. God, it looked even worse than the last time I'd been here. "And who's this?"

She smiled at Andre and bent forward to give him a clear shot of her cleavage.

Oh. My. Sweet. Jesus. He gave me penthouse suite Valentine romance, and I gave him white trash wedding.

"This is Andre." I smoothed a hand over my skirt to make it wasn't hiked up around my waist still. We'd cleaned up in the car after our dirty little sexfest, but this was *so* not the way to enjoy orgasmic afterglow.

He nodded to my aunt. "Madame."

Her grin widened as she took in his limo and expensive suit. Her hair was limp and dirty, and her nose was red and raw. She twitched and sniffled constantly.

I swallowed, but grinned as wide as I could at him and laid a hand on his chest. "You don't have to come in. I just want to check on Desi."

What I wanted was to get my little cousin the hell out of this shit hole, but that wouldn't happen. I took a deep breath and nearly gagged on the stink of this place. Ragged weeds grew

Crystal Jordan

everywhere, and I was pretty sure there were landmines of dog poo hiding in the yard.

His voice was low enough so that only I could hear while he offered an impersonal smile to Misty. "Nonsense. I won't leave you here alone."

"She's my aunt. Nothing bad will happen."

"And she'll pull you up when you fall through the floor?"

Good point. I'm about three times my aunt's height and twice her weight. No way in hell could she help me up. Then again, I have a vampire's strength now, I could get up by myself. But...I *wanted* him with me. "Fine."

His hand settled warm on the small of my back, and even that simple touch made tingles shoot up my spine. "After you, *cherie*."

I lead the way into the double-wide. The steps groaned under Andre's weight as he came up behind me. If I was a big girl, he was a huge man. The only man I knew even close to his size was Michael.

"Cyn, I totally thought that was you!" Desi launched herself at me as soon as I cleared the front door.

I hugged her tightly to reassure myself that she was okay. God, I'd been so damn scared. A huge weight lifted from my chest, and tears of relief pressed hard against my eyelids. I took a shuddering breath. Then I held her at arm's length so I could look at her, make certain she really was okay.

She had a black eye that I hoped to God was from the crash. My heart squeezed to see it. Other than that, she looked fine. Her curly mop of black hair and *café au lait* skin set off her Trent-blue eyes. Michael, Misty and I had the same eyes.

No one knows who Desi's dad was. Not even Misty. Probably one of her johns on his sloppy thirds.

Desi looked a lot like what I imagined Andre and my babies would look like. Not that I wanted to bear his undead offspring. Of course not.

Okay, maybe a little.

Could vampires even have children? I'd never asked anyone before because I was so freaked about the bride of Satan thing. I made a mental note to ask Andre or Candy, but Desi was talking a mile a minute, so I focused on her. Her sentences were peppered with *dude, like, totally, whatever,* and *as if.* I was a little worried that she picked up some of those speech patterns from me. But whatever.

Her eyes popped wide when she peeked around me and saw Andre. I tensed. *Shit.* To someone as teensy as Desi, Andre would be a big, scary motherfucker. The long fangs wouldn't help at all.

He squatted down in front of her to bring himself to her eye level. *"Bonjour,* Desi. I'm Andre."

She clung to my hand and ducked shyly behind me. "Hi."

"I'm Cyn's friend." His voice was low and gentle. My heart squeezed so tight, I knew that's when I fell completely in love with him. The rest had built to this, but now I was certain. I was a little slow on the uptake, yeah, but seeing him try so hard for me was all I needed. This was a man who would do anything for me, including walk into a shit-infested trailer park, deal with a drunk-ass hooker and make friends with a little girl. Just to make me happy.

Shit, now I was gonna cry for a whole different reason.

"Cyn's my favorite."

He flicked his gaze up to mine as he smiled. "Mine too."

Desi's signature grin exploded across her face and lit her up. Her free hand caught his, and she pulled us over to the couch, smushing in between us.

Misty flopped into a broken recliner that sagged in the middle, a fresh bottle of Jack Daniels in her hand. Alcohol dribbled down her chin as she took a swig straight from the bottle. My stomach roiled at the thought of leaving Desi alone here, and I glanced away. My gaze collided with Andre's over Desi's head. Understanding softened his face. Yeah, he got it.

He cleared his throat and looked at Misty. She leered at him.

"You have a...cozy home."

"Yeah, I used to have a big house—nice—before my old man left me. Before I popped that one out." She jerked her chin at Desi.

His voice remained pleasant. "You'd like that again? A large house?"

My breath caught. What was he doing?

She narrowed her eyes, glanced at me, then leaned toward him so she almost fell out of tube top she wore. "What are you suggesting...Andre, right?"

"Just that a relation so...*beloved* to my Cynthiana should have whatever she desires."

"What're you getting at?" Her chin tilted, and I could almost hear the alcohol-greased gears spin in her head.

He shrugged and smiled with easy charm. "I have a mansion in Los Angeles. I would love to have you and Desiree come stay with us. Of course, you would have everything you wanted provided to you by my servants."

Greed lit her eyes, and it disgusted me to see it. If Andre had offered, I bet Misty would have sold Desi to him for the price of a new bottle of booze and an ounce of blow. That was a tactic I hadn't tried before. Of course, I didn't have the resources Andre did.

"Everything I want?"

"Of course. There is a condition."

"A catch? You can't throw in a catch now!" Her eyes bulged, and she sloshed liquor down her front as she sat up.

"It's an easy condition. You and Desi have to come with us today. Now."

"Now?"

"Yes. Pack your things and come with us. That simple. What will it be?"

My breath froze. A huge hand fisted around my ribs and squeezed tight. Oh, God, please. Please. Let this work. Let us get Desi away from this place and give her a fighting chance. If Misty came willingly, then there was no need to go through the court system or deal with vampire-human adoption. Or at least California was a more liberal state than Nevada about that kind of thing. And maybe, I dared to hope, maybe Misty would clean up if she got away from here too. All the thoughts swirled in my head and made me dizzy. That and the lack of oxygen. I sucked in a huge breath.

Please, please, please, please.

"Okay."

The air whooshed out of my lungs. Did she just say...? She didn't...

"Excellent." Andre turned to me. "Why don't you help Desi pack her things while I settle on the details with your aunt?"

I nodded like a bobblehead doll on speed. Anything. Anything for this to be real. "Okay. Sure."

Taking Desi's hand, I stood and pulled her to the back of the trailer. The flimsy floor creaked under me as we went.

"Cyn? Does this mean I get to live with you now?"

Um. Wait. Andre asked them to move in with him, but I don't live with him. *Shit.* That was a little wrinkle to iron out, but frankly I'd cohabit with the real Satan if it got me Desi. "I think so, honey."

"Will Beelzebub come too?"

"He goes where I go."

"And Mom?" She dropped to the filthy carpet and rummaged under her bed. The room was beyond Spartan. It was just empty. Barren. I squared my shoulders. That was easy enough to fix.

"Yep."

She shimmied out, and a Barbie suitcase came with her. Plopping it open on her little bed, she ran around and scooped clothes off the floor and out of drawers. What she had didn't even fill the tiny case. She paused in her frantic packing to turn back to me. "And Andre?"

Live with Andre? My stomach fluttered with terror and excitement. This was huge, but not bad. I sighed and let a small smile break out. "All of us."

"Even Michael?"

I chuckled at the mental picture of my brother living under Andre's roof. Yeah, that would so work. "No, but he lives in L.A. too. Nearby."

"What about my friend Lindsay?"

"No, she has to stay here with her parents."

Her little face scrunched up. "Oh. I'll miss her though."

"I know, baby." I knelt down and hugged her tight.

"Will I see her anymore?"

"I don't know. There will be other kids in your new school and in Andre's neighborhood."

"Nice kids? Not everyone is nice." Her wide blue eyes were a little too wise and knowing about the cruelty of humans. God, I would fight until I dropped to protect her from now on. I knew

Andre would too. And Michael and Candy. My best friend would love Desi, though she'd pop a vein when she heard about Andre. This would be too...interesting.

"Can I go say goodbye to Lindsay?" Desi pulled me from my thoughts.

I stroked a hand down her curls. "Sure, honey. Meet me at the car in twenty minutes."

"I'm gonna tell her I get a mansion!" Her grin lit up her face as her natural enthusiasm bubbled up. She raced for the door, skipping and bouncing as she went. It made me laugh to see her.

Hefting her little suitcase, I walked toward the front door. I passed Misty's room on the way to see her stuff her clothing into Hefty bags. "Where's Andre?"

"How should I know? I'm busy." She grunted each time she jumped to reach for shoeboxes on the top shelf of her closet. I could have reached them for her, but I had to talk to Andre. Right now.

"Okay." I backed out and closed the door. The search was on for my tall, dark and undead hero. I grinned.

It was easy to find him. He leaned against the hood of the limo, head down, shoulders hunched, arms crossed over his chest.

"Well, that's one strategy to get a girl to move in with you."

He sighed and rubbed his hand over the back of his neck. "You don't have to stay in the same room with me. I have a huge house. I'm sorry, Cynthiana. I took over. Again. Without asking you. *Merde.*"

"Andre—"

"In my defense, this is new for me, *cherie*. I'll get better, I swear. I am trying. I—"

"I know."

His mouth snapped closed, then opened again. "You do?"

I set Desi's suitcase down and stepped forward to wrap my arms around his waist. His hands dropped to cup my hips. "I trust you to not do anything to deliberately hurt me. I have a lot to learn too. About trusting someone besides myself. I'm not very good at it."

"Will you try...with me?"

"*Je t'aime.*" I know I butchered the accent, but he got the message because his body went rigid against mine. I pulled back to look him in the eye. "It means I love you, doesn't it?"

"*Oui.*" He squeezed me so tight, my breath rushed out.

"You've said it since the first time we slept together."

"I've meant it since then. I turned you because I felt it. There will never be another woman for me, *cherie*. I would give you the world if I could."

"I only want you." I grinned. "And Desi, but you made that happen for me."

"Anything. If it's within my power. Anything."

I laid my cheek against his chest, felt his heart hammer. Contentment wound through me and filled me up. This was it. This was what I wanted. "I love you, Andre. I don't know about the rest, but I'm sure of that."

"*Je t'aime aussi, cherie.* Forever."

And who would know more about forever than a vampire? It sounded...perfect to me. It wouldn't be easy with Desi and Misty and the two of us. We had a very long road ahead of us, but we'd work all of it out. We had plenty of time.

"Forever," I agreed.

It's Raining Men

Dedication

For my girls: R.G. Alexander, Eden Bradley, Loribelle Hunt, Lillian Feisty, Dayna Hart, Jennifer Leeland and Bethany Morgan.

Chapter One

Oh God. Kill me now.

I fought the urge to bury my head in my hands—or toss back the rest of my double shot of bourbon—as I saw who walked in the door of the Eclipse bar. It was my birthday, damn it. My *thirty-first* birthday. As in, no longer just thirty, but *in my thirties.* Why couldn't I spend it in peace?

Yeah, yeah. As a werewolf, I'd live a couple hundred years. I knew that. But the last few years had seemed to crawl by in one endless string of pain. It was the feeling that werewolves who denied themselves their mates dealt with. Pain. Bone-crushing, head-throbbing, drop-me-to-my-knees aguish.

And my *unclaimed* mate had just stepped into the room, so I felt it with the keen agony of the sharpest blade. Michael Trent. Older brother of my best friend, Cynthiana Trent-St. James. Why would she bring him here?

Eclipse was a place I thought I'd be safe. Only magical creatures came here. Humans who ventured in were just asking to be an after-dinner snack for something that went bump in the night. Or some*one*. Someone like me. And my best-friend-turned-traitor. *Not* like her very human brother. I'd managed to avoid running into him for months now. Damn Cyn for forcing this.

"Hey, sexy." Cyn tugged on one of my curls, making it bounce against my neck. A low, warning growl vibrated my vocal cords as she slid into the chair on my left. The sound ended in a whimper when Michael settled his big, scrumptious self into the seat on my right. The tiny table and cramped space meant his muscular thigh and arm were plastered against mine.

My sex throbbed at the benign contact, my nipples peaking tight as my instincts screamed in a desperate attempt to encourage me to claim him. To remind me how phenomenal sex was supposed to be with a mate. My body heated from the inside out, goose bumps shivering over my skin when he shifted his leg and leaned closer to me. "Happy birthday, Candy. You look good enough to eat in that dress. I'm not sure if that makes you Little Red Riding Hood or the Big Bad Wolf."

His deep voice caressed my heightened hearing, his breath moving the tiny hairs at my temple. I shuddered and fought to keep myself from throwing him to the ground to have my way with him. Even though he was three times my size, my werewolf strength could easily best even the biggest human. Big Bad Wolf, indeed. I tugged at the hem of my short, tight scarlet silk dress. I mean, I liked my ample curves just fine, but they didn't need to be falling out for the world to see. The top of this thing was about to give up the fight with my breasts, and I was pretty sure when I stood my *assets* would be hanging out the back.

"Ha! I designed that outfit for her present." Cyn ran a proprietary hand over the beading on my shoulder strap, her fashion-designer self geeking out over her creation. "Doesn't she look hot?"

"Oh. Yeah." He gave me the kind of once-over that had made my heart leap in my chest since the first time I met him. I hadn't known then that when the sharp, intimidating prosecutor left the courtroom he was an incorrigible flirt. The pain that plagued me every single time I denied the need to sink my fangs into his flesh and mark him as *mine* gave an especially vicious twist.

"You should ask her to dance." Cyn gestured to postage-sized dance floor in front of the stage where couples were locked in the kind of embraces that only Saran Wrap could maintain.

If I slammed my pointy high heel down on her toe, who would blame me? She knew that Michael was my mate, and she took every opportunity to throw me in his path. She wanted me to hook up with her brother, but it wasn't going to happen for two very big reasons. First, when Cyn's husband Andre turned her into a vampire last year, he didn't exactly ask her permission first. Magical people had a bad rap as it was, since the fighting between wolves and vamps had dragged every single species, from sprite to necromancer, out into the light of day about a decade ago. Well, vampires never made it out into the light of day, but that was beside the point. Michael, being the overprotective human brother, was more than a little bent out of shape about his little sister getting turned into a bloodsucker. Even now, with Cyn and Andre happily ensconced in some overpriced mansion in Bel Air, Michael had serious reservations about magical beings. Like me.

But the biggest reason why Michael and I would never find true love was one I was sure his sister didn't know about. The day Cyn introduced me to him, and I sensed he was meant to be mine forever, I tracked him to his house and found him getting hot and heavy with another man. Yeah, that was great. I was not going to be the one to break it to my best friend that her big, manly brother was *gay*.

As in, not into chicks.

As in, never going to mate with me, and I was going to spend every birthday alone for the rest of my long, long life.

"I need another drink."

Chapter Two

My chair tumbled to the floor as I shot to my feet. Michael rose with me, his hand burning into the small of my back. "Are you sure you need another drink, Candy?"

"Oh yeah." I needed to get away from this table was what I needed. Every instinct lit as his palm stroked up my back to settle on my bare shoulder. He turned me toward him, and his arm wrapped around me. His strong fingers kneaded the nape of my neck. That familiar flirtatious smile curved his lips, an invitation to something I knew he wouldn't be interested in following through on. But my body didn't care. All it noticed was the way the calluses on his fingers stimulated my flesh. I swallowed, my lids drooping to half-mast. My claws bit into my palms as I clenched my fists. I could feel the pointed tips of my fangs press against my closed lips. I wanted him in every possible way—in my life, in my bed, by my side. Forever. The wolf within me snapped and clawed for freedom, demanding to claim what belonged to it. Michael.

Dragging in a steadying breath I caught the scent of his heady, masculine smell. His spicy cologne mixed with an aroma that would always be *his*. Every second his skin touched mine sent moisture pooling between my thighs. I squeezed them together, but it did nothing to quiet the intense need that whipped through me. Molten heat flowed like lava through my veins, melting everything in its path. I wanted nothing more than to lose myself in the sensations my mate awoke in me. To lose myself in the love that had grown deeper and hotter with every passing day since I'd met him.

The opening cords of music pumped from the sound system in the bar. Michael leaned in to speak in my ear. "Do you want me to get it for you? What would you like?"

I'd like him naked and pumping his cock inside me until I burned off this craving I had for his big, muscular body. Until I forgot how much I loved his smile, his sense of humor, his protective nature. Hell, until I forgot my own name. I released a shuddering breath and stepped away from the almost irresistible temptation he presented. "No, I...I can handle it myself. Thanks."

Scooting around my fallen chair, I spun towards the long wooden bar that held my only reprieve for the evening. Booze. I needed another shot glass full of joy juice to make it through this. My body still hummed from being in close proximity to Michael. The desire was almost unbearable, and I fought a whimper. Each step made my thighs brush together, and reminded me how much I ached to be touched, to be filled. By Michael. The thought was hot enough to make my breath catch.

Then, just to make my night a little more fun, the crowd shifted and I saw the man talking to the bartender. My boss, Malcon. Who also happened to be the werewolf pack Alpha in Los Angeles. I was the executive chef for the pack leaders. Collectively, they ran a very successful international corporation, which meant a lot of work for me. It also meant I saw more than enough of the powerful people in my world going through those business headquarters every day, but it figured Malcon would be here. He'd become fast friends with the werewolf owners of the neutral-territory bar since he had assumed leadership and declared that wolves in *his* pack would no longer be allowed to engage in the war with vampires. It made me like him as a person since my best friend just happened to be a bloodsucker, but that didn't mean I wanted to hang out with him tonight. He was *my boss* and *the Alpha*, after all. He hadn't seen me yet, and I wasn't about to call myself to his attention. Switching directions, I darted through the crowd towards the ladies' room. I needed to cool off and settle down before I dealt with anyone.

The restroom was empty, thank you sweet baby Jesus. I stumbled to the counter and leaned my shaking hands on either side of one of the sinks. Drawing in slow, deep breaths, I tried to reach for the calm that I'd perfected for the times I couldn't avoid my best friend's brother. It didn't come.

"Shit." I glanced up in the mirror and met my own desperate gaze. The pupils seemed to dominate the dark irises, and my dark hair set off the deep flush in my cheeks. I closed my eyes, not wanting to see the evidence of my need stamped so clearly on my features. But it only brought my other senses to the fore, and the hint of Michael's scent beckoned me. I shuddered as lust speared me, my claws erupting to scrape the countertop. The wolf fought for supremacy. When my eyes snapped open, I could see they'd burned to pure, icy blue.

My jaw clenched as resignation slid through me. I couldn't go back out there this way, and I couldn't bail on my own birthday. Turning my back on the mirror, I walked into one of the stalls and locked the door behind me. Concentrating on my hand, I managed to retract my claws. The pads of my fingers brushed over my knee as I slid the hem of my dress up. My breath hissed between my teeth. Any relief from the desire pulsing through me was enough to make my legs shake. My forehead rested against the cool tile wall, and the contrast to my overheating flesh had me biting my lip to keep in a whimper. Please, don't let anyone walk in here.

I never wore panties, and tonight was no exception. The first touch against my swollen clit made me jolt. Tingles erupted down my arms and legs. I swallowed as my fingers slipped into my hot channel. Plunging in quick, hard strokes, I couldn't keep Michael's face from flashing through my mind. Pleasure arced through my body like lightning. My mate often featured in my fantasies. I couldn't help it... I didn't want to.

Closing my eyes, I could picture him so clearly. His big body rose behind me, surrounding me as he took over stroking my slick flesh. My mouth opened in a silent scream as he spun me against the wall, lifted me and plunged his cock inside me. The stretch was exquisite pain, and he worked me with brutal speed. He whispered my name as we rode each other. My pussy flexed around his dick as reality and fantasy blurred, and there was nothing left but pure need. Yes. I wanted it to be real so badly, wanted him to fuck me until I thought I'd die from the pleasure.

My thighs eased farther apart, and my breath rushed in harsh pants as I held on to the dream for a moment longer. The wetness increased as I dropped my other hand to press my thumb against my hardened clit. My hips rolled in an erotic rhythm I couldn't stop. I was so close, I could feel the contractions building deep in my belly, clenching my pussy around my fingers.

"Michael," I breathed, and crashed into the wall of my orgasm. I shuddered over and over again, a low moan ripping from my throat.

The door to the bathroom squeaked open, and I caught my breath. Reality returned with a rude jolt. I froze, my fangs popping out as the wolf sensed a threat. My nostrils flared to catch the intruder's scent. Not another wolf, nor a vampire. Fae, probably. I heard the slight flutter of wings. Yep, I was right...a fairy. So, whoever she was, she wouldn't be able to sense me, or smell the slight musk of sex in the room. Thank heavens.

I shivered and jerked my hand from under my dress, pulling it down. Jesus, I was going insane. Look what I'd been reduced to, getting my rocks off in a public bathroom stall. Shame flushed my cheeks. What was *wrong* with me? Oh, wait. I had a gay man for a mate. That was enough to drive any wolf nutty. I sighed and closed my eyes. The lingering pleasure of orgasm evaporated under the unrelenting sadness that never seemed to leave me. I swallowed hard and blinked back the sudden tears that sheened my eyes. It wouldn't change anything to cry about it, so I sucked in a breath and forced the lonely grief deep, deep down, the way I always did. If I let it take over, it had the power to cripple me, and I might not be able to function.

The fairy woman left, and the door screeched shut behind her. I sagged against the tile wall, exhaustion crashing over me. Wasn't my birthday over *yet*?

Stepping out of the stall, I washed my hands in the sink and splashed cool water on my flushed cheeks. I didn't bother looking in the mirror—I just didn't want to know. Wiping my hands and face with a paper towel, I crumpled the brown paper, tossed it in the wastebasket and followed the fairy out the door.

I didn't really want a drink now, I just wanted to go home, but I approached the long wooden bar anyway. Time to paste on a smile and put on a good show for my best friend.

Jerrod, one of the werewolf owners of Eclipse, worked like a well-oiled machine behind the bar. He had on a black wifebeater and jeans that hugged his big, well-muscled frame. Thankfully, Malcon had disappeared, so I didn't have to deal with him. Jerrod's midnight blue eyes crinkled at the corners, and he smiled as I stepped up to order. "Candy girl, you are looking luscious in that dress tonight."

"You're always welcome to look, hot stuff." I ran a hand down the red silk covering my hip and winked at him. A grin bloomed on my lips. Flirting with Jerrod was too much fun. Mostly because he was safely mated to *two* she-wolves. His cup overfloweth on the mate front. Unlike most men, he wouldn't expect me to follow through on anything. I hadn't been able to since I met Michael. No other man would do. Just the thought was enough to make me physically ill. There was no infidelity for werewolves—it just didn't work for my kind. Apparently, my instincts decided I didn't even have to *be* mated to remain faithful.

Jerrod ran his tongue down a canine tooth. "What's your pleasure tonight, Candy?"

"I'd like a scotch, neat." I avoided the too-knowing look in his eyes by scanning the crowd in Eclipse. One of Jerrod's mates, Rachel, set a cocktail on a table near the front door. His other mate, Lena, stepped through the bar's entrance just then, and her eyes lit up when she saw Rachel. The two women embraced and gave each other a slow kiss. I could feel their passion for each other from here. They both turned for the bar, that same look of love and lust on their faces when they smiled at Jerrod. I sighed. "You're a lucky man, Jerrod."

"I know it." He handed me my drink, but when I glanced back at him, he only had eyes for his mates. "Happy birthday, Candy. It's on the house."

Was it bad that I was enough of a regular here they knew it was my birthday?

"Thanks." Not bothering to argue, I took my scotch and ran before the lovefest began with the three mates. I was just not ready to deal with that tonight, so I hurried back to the table. Would they notice I'd been gone too long? The only thing I could be thankful for was that none of them was a wolf—they didn't have enhanced senses to smell the fact that I'd just had a little self-lovefest in the bathroom.

In my rush to get back, I damn near plowed Cyn's husband over. It looked like Andre had arrived in time for my party of pain. His hands snapped around my shoulders to catch me before I stumbled.

"Candace." His celery green gaze searched my face. "What's wrong, *petite*?"

I couldn't quite meet his eyes. Andre had been around for a few centuries at least. He always saw more than I was comfortable with. I forced a wide grin to my lips. "Everything's fine, Andre."

"You're certain?" His French Creole accent rolled like smooth honey, and his teeth flashed white against his chocolate skin as he offered me a reassuring smile. The smile turned positively wicked when his gaze shifted from me to my best friend.

"Totally sure." Shrugging out of his grasp, I plopped into my chair and took a deep drink of my scotch.

Andre and Cyn kissed, and I kept my gaze pinned to the stage that a small army of men swarmed around, taking down musical equipment from the last band and setting up equipment for the next act. I didn't want to watch my friend's happy reunion with her husband. I didn't want to be jealous of how happy she was with her new undeath, but I was. Yeah, I knew it made me an asshole, and guilt pinched my insides. It twisted within me, tightening around the ever-present frustration and sadness. I couldn't help it—I just wanted to be happy too. And I never would be. I'd always be wishing for what could never be. That Michael would love me the way I loved him. Hopelessly, endlessly. Damn it.

"Stephen Parthon's about to start." Cyn slid back into the seat beside me, sandwiching me between her and Michael again. I refused to look at him. Andre sat on Cyn's other side, and their clasped hands rested on the tabletop.

"W-what?" I finally met her gaze, but had no clue what she was talking about.

She gave me the kind of look reserved for kids that rode the short bus to school. "Stephen. Parthon. The half-Fae, half-siren jazz singer you were so excited to listen to you blew off my surprise party to see him?"

"Surprise parties are supposed to be a surprise. How was I to know you planned one?" I gave her a more genuine smile than any I'd managed this evening and took a sip of my drink.

"Don't insult my intelligence." She gave me a sharp smile, complete with a little baring of vampire fangs. "Lucky for you, I'm a great friend, and I brought the party to you."

I stuck my tongue out at her. "There went my great escape."

Not a scrap of sympathy shone on her face. "Suck it up."

"Vampires are the ones who suck, haven't you heard?" It was part of our relationship to harass each other, and we were really good at it. Like sisters...or so I imagined. I was an only child, and both my parents were long dead. Having Cyn was *almost* like having family again, and I treasured that. It was nice to know there was someone in the world looking out for me and making sure I didn't fall through the cracks. Even if we did pester the crap out of each other most of the time. I leaned my shoulder against her, and she hugged me with her free arm, resting her chin on top of my head.

"Happy birthday, wolf breath. I love you."

A watery chuckle was the only response I could manage. Thankfully, the lights went up on the stage, and the slow, hypnotic beat of a drum drowned out anything I might have said.

Chapter Three

An unassuming man with short-cropped brown curls walked on to the stage and slouched down on the stool. He adjusted the microphone and looked over at the saxophone player. A small smile played over his lips as his gaze swept the crowd. The most intense emerald green eyes met mine, and I straightened a little. When he opened his mouth, the low, smoky note was the most beautiful thing I'd ever heard. It brought me completely upright, and I leaned forward in my chair, enraptured.

The saxophone and drums swelled to compliment that stunning voice. They wove together, toying with each other in a sweet melody. It grabbed me, sank deep into my soul and soothed the part of me that ached. I closed my eyes, knowing that this man, this stranger, understood my pain the way no one else ever had before. The loneliness that defined my childhood, the shattering anguish of losing my family, the endless agony of having a mate I couldn't claim. But he also understood my joy, the love I had for my friends, the family I *made* rather than the one I was born to, my career as a chef. It was there in that voice, in the lyrics, in the smooth, deep tone that caressed my sensitive ears. For the first time in forever, the wolf within me quieted, content to rest.

"I've never heard a siren sing before. It's everything they said and more. Captivating." Cyn's voice reached my ears as one song ended and another began, and I opened my eyes to find tears sliding down my cheeks. I swiped them away, glad the lights were dim.

I coughed and took a swig of my scotch. Captivating, yes. That was the perfect word for it. Dragging in a deep breath, I propped my chin in my palm as I scanned the crowd. The cacophony that was typical of Eclipse was gone. Every single person stared at the stage, at Stephen Parthon, enthralled. His voice was the only sound to be heard.

The song wound to a close, and the siren spoke for the first time. "Good evening, everyone. We have a...special request tonight. There's someone celebrating a birthday in the crowd."

Oh God. Please don't let him be talking about me. *Please* let someone else here be having a birthday.

Yeah, I'm so not that lucky.

"Candy, why don't you stand up so we can wish you a happy birthday?"

I pinched my eyes closed for a moment, praying for death. Or at least a gaping hole to open up in the floor and swallow me. I hissed under my breath, "What part of *I don't want to make a big deal of my birthday* was too difficult for you all to understand?"

"Blame me if you you're going to get mad. But get up and get it over with." Michael swatted my ass hard when I stood, and the crowd hooted. He raised his voice to be heard above them. "That's one to grow on, birthday girl!"

That got another cheer from the crowd, and Stephen chuckled into the microphone as he stepped off the stage and approached our table. A hot flushed washed up my cheeks, then rushed out fast enough to make my face tingle. As a chef, I was always behind the scenes. I didn't like to be the center of attention, especially for this. Stephen sang a smooth jazz rendition of *Happy Birthday to You.* His gaze caught mine, and I was irresistibly drawn in to those emerald depths. I swayed towards him, forgetting all about the crowd. Sirens...wow. I'd never reacted to one this way, but I didn't care. I just wanted to listen to him forever.

His gaze never left mine as he backed toward the stage, sitting on the edge. I took that as my cue to take my seat, and I leaned back, letting my hands fall to my lap. He segued from my birthday ballad to a song about love and wild, maddening lust. A smile that was ten kinds of wicked flashed across his face. It made an answering grin curl the corner of my lips as a surprising heat built inside me. I hadn't reacted to anyone except Michael with cold indifference since the day I met him. But I couldn't deny Stephen's words of longing and fiery passion made my toes curl in my pointy heels. My nipples peaked hard, and the way his smile turned flirtatious made it clear he loved what his voice could do to a woman. I drew in a shuddering breath, my heart picking up speed until I could hear the pulse of it in my ears.

A shiver ran through my body when Michael's callused fingertips slid over the back of my hand. I flushed for an entirely different reason, thankful that his actions were hidden by the table so Cyn wouldn't know. My thighs clenched together as he drew slow patterns on my skin, raising goose bumps up my arms. I should pull my hand away, I knew. But I couldn't make myself. Not tonight. I needed...something. The restless ache that gnawed at me had built to a fever pitch today, and I just couldn't force myself to deny my mate's touch. Just this, just for now. A shudder ran through Michael's big body as the song continued, and I could smell the way my own desire melded with his. His shoulder brushed against me, and his fingers toyed with mine.

Stephen's gaze slid back and forth between Michael and me, the sinful glint in his eyes showing he knew exactly what effect his voice had on us. Heat wound through me, battering at my control. The wolf in me was suddenly awake, alert. I barely managed to bite back a helpless moan. Time stretched out as one song after another played, revving my body up with longing. I could stay like this all night, Michael petting me, Stephen singing to me.

Cyn's cell phone lit up and rattled across the tabletop as it vibrated. Michael and I jolted. His hand left my skin, and we both turned to look at his sister. She scooped up the phone and gave us an apologetic look. Pushing a button, she pressed it to her ear. "Hello?"

Concern sharpened her features, and her hand came down on Andre's forearm. I faced her fully and both men came to full attention, leaning toward Cyn. "Are you sure? No, no. It's fine. Andre and I can come home."

Andre was already pulling bills from his wallet, more than enough to cover the drinks on the table, and pushing his chair back. "What is happening, *cherie*?"

She flicked the phone closed with her chin and looked at me. "Looks like you're being spared more birthday torture. Desi's come down with something and is throwing up. My aunt is freaking, so we're going to head home and clean up the mess."

"Is she okay? Maybe I should come with you." Michael moved as if to rise, and both Andre and Cyn waved him back down. The two vampires had taken in Cyn and Michael's young human cousin while at the same time helping their druggie aunt get clean. It had been pretty rocky at first, but things had been going well for the last few months. I adored Desi and hoped this little emergency didn't derail her mom's progress.

127

Cyn tucked her phone into her handbag. "We can handle this. There's been a stomach bug going around at her school lately, so I'm sure it's fine." Bending forward to kiss my cheek, she hugged me good-bye. "Happy birthday, honey. Sorry to leave you two alone. Can you make sure she gets home safe, Michael?"

"Of course." His hand bracketed the back of my neck, and he heaved a long-suffering, put-upon sigh. "I'll drive her home so she can have another three or four whiskeys if she wants."

I rolled my eyes. "I'm *not* drunk, Michael. Just because your sister is a total lightweight doesn't mean all women are."

"Well, now you can drink like the heavyweight champ you are. You have a designated driver." He grinned down at me, massaging my nape in slow circles. I shivered and jerked my gaze back to Cyn. But the vampires were already hurrying for the door, people stepping out of Andre's path at just a look from the big man.

The music from the stage came to a slow close, and Stephen spoke into the mic. "Well, folks, that's all for the evening. Thank you for coming. Let's have a hand for my band and for the amazing owners of the best magical bar in town."

He led the crowd in raucous applause as his bandmates took a bow and Rachel, Lena and Jerrod waved from behind the bar. Then the siren sketched a quick bow himself and the crowd leaped to their feet and screamed. Michael and I were no exception. We both stood and clapped hard. Stephen flashed a quick smile, gave a jaunty little wiggle of his fingers and jumped off the stage to head straight for our table.

"Hey, you." Stephen walked up and wrapped his hand around the back of Michael's neck, pulling him forward for a kiss.

I blinked and stared at them. They broke apart and turned to face me. Stephen leaned back against Michael's broad chest,

128

but gave me that same wicked smile he'd given me from the stage and an obvious once-over. My eyebrows arched in surprise. "Um..."

"Candy, I'd like you to meet Stephen. Stephen, this is Candy." Michael grinned at me, not a hint of embarrassment on his face. He was comfortable in his own skin, in his sexuality, and I couldn't help but think it made him sexier. It just meant he still wasn't for me. Damn it. "Candy's my sister's best friend and the head chef for the werewolf pack leaders."

"Sounds tasty." The Fae-siren man slid his hand into mine, his fingers warm and strong. "Candy."

A mischievous twinkle flashed in his eyes, so common a look among the Fae. A fairy who was a *fairy*. I wished it was funnier than it was. I mostly just wanted to cry as he leaned into Michael's embrace.

Michael's laser blue gaze bore into me, and I could only hope I had a better poker face than I thought I did. "It's interesting that you wanted to see Stephen perform since I've been...ah, *seeing him perform* for a few months now."

"Interesting. Yeah." Why didn't the Earth just open up and swallow me whole now? *I'm ready to go now, God.* It couldn't possibly get worse than this.

And then it did.

Chapter Four

Stephen's hand slid out of mine, his fingertips stroking over my palm. My instincts gave a painful jolt just then, burning away what was left of my alcohol-induced buzz.

Mate. Stephen. *Mate.*

Holy shit on a shingle.

It couldn't be. I refused to believe it. There had to be something seriously out of whack with my instincts if they were telling me I was supposed to claim *two* men as my mate. Two *gay* men. Who were not just gay, but gay *together.* A hysterical laugh bubbled up in my throat, tangling with a sob before it could erupt. Oh God, I wanted to die. The ripping, tearing agony I felt when I was near Michael sliced through me—like a double-edged sword, it cut both ways. Stephen, Michael. Michael, Stephen. My instincts flashed like strobe lights in recognition.

Stepping away from them, I tried to offer a smile. It fell like a bad soufflé. "Well...um. I'll leave you to your evening. I think I've had enough birthday for one year."

Get me out of here. That's all I could think. This was more than I could handle. I was done. So, *so* very done. Snagging my bag off the back of my chair, I slid the strap over my shoulder and turned around to walk away. I *needed* to walk away. All I wanted was for Michael to be happy. Hell, for *both* of my mates to be happy. But I didn't have to stay around and watch their warm fuzzy moments unfold for them. I got no more than three steps before a hard, masculine hand wrapped around my elbow and pulled me to a stop. Resisting the urge to use my werewolf strength to rip my arm free of his grasp, I shot a glare over my shoulder at Michael.

He let me go and lifted both hands in supplication. "Sorry, Candy. I can't let you leave without me. I promised my sister I'd drive you home."

"I'm not drunk, Michael, but if it makes you feel better, I can take a cab home."

Stephen stepped up behind Michael, pulling a leather jacket on over his black T-shirt. "You think you're going to get a cab in this neighborhood at this time of night? I doubt it, gorgeous. Just let us take you home. It's no problem."

The amount of charm in his smile was enough to drown me. I had to shake myself and look away, reminding myself that both sides of this man's nature were meant to ensnare and enchant people. Being a magical creature myself didn't make me immune to it. A sigh slid out of my lips. I could stand here and argue with them and maybe not be able to get a cab, or I could give in now and endure twenty minutes in Michael's SUV to escape for good. No contest. "Fine. Let's go. Thanks."

I didn't look at them, just headed for the door. My stomach churned with each step. The scotch threatened to come back up at any moment. Too bad, it would be a waste of good alcohol. I swallowed hard and stepped out into the warm Southern California night air, pulling in a deep breath. Along with the smog, it brought both men's scents deep into my lungs. My insides clenched, then softened as though preparing for the kind of possession my inner wolf craved. Two mates nearby had it howling. I rolled my eyes at myself. *Down, girl.*

"Where did you park?" I stopped at the curb, and Stephen walked right into me. His arms snapped around me before my high heels made me teeter into the street. My breath caught as his ropey muscles seared into my back. His hands pressed to my ribs, just under my breasts. My nipples went hard and tight, fire pumping through my veins as my heart slammed in my chest. When I felt his impressive erection nudge against my backside, my jaw locked and my fangs slid down. I knew if either man looked at me, they would see my eyes had gone pale blue as the wolf wrestled for control. I shuddered and covered Stephen's forearms with my palms. "I have my balance." Liar— I'd never been so off-kilter. "You can let go now." *Or throw me to the ground and fuck me hard. I'm open.*

"The SUV is half a block up and across the street." Michael's hand slid down my arm, pulling it away from Stephen to link our fingers. Stephen slipped his hand into my free one and the three of us jogged across the street. Now that I was on this side of the road, I could see Michael's sleek silver vehicle. He opened the passenger-side door for me, and both men helped me into the supple leather seat.

Michael loped around to the driver's side while Stephen slid into the middle of the backseat and leaned between the front seats to grin at both of us. "Well, then. Do you know where we're going, Michael?"

"Yeah. I've driven Cyn over to Candy's place a few times." He winked in the rearview mirror at Stephen, started the car and smoothly pulled out into the late-night traffic. He drove with quiet confidence, maneuvering through the intersections and cutting through side streets on the way to my condo.

I watched his hands stroke the steering wheel and wished they were stroking me instead. Swallowing, I glanced back at Stephen. "So...how did you two meet?"

Michael chuckled. "At a gala ball for the mayor. Stephen was singing at the party, and I was there mingling for political reasons."

Stephen took up the thread of the story. "And I walked right up to him and said, 'Do you believe in love at first sight?' He smiled and said no, so I told him he'd have to get to know me so he could catch up, because I believed."

"That's sweet." I forced out the words. It was true...I just wished it wasn't.

"Okay, Michael, you're going to have to take me somewhere to get something to eat. I have a serious case of the munchies. I always get this way after a performance." Stephen's endless energy made it seem like he was always in motion, even when he sat still. It was the exact opposite of Michael, who had an amazing *stillness*, an intensity that drew people to him. In their own ways, they both drew people like moths to open flames. I sighed. They certainly drew me in.

I stared out the passenger window, trying hard not to pay attention to them. Please, let this be over soon. I could strip off the teeny-tiny dress and get into my most comfortable pair of pajamas. Curled up on my big leather sofa with a bowl of my homemade vanilla-bean ice cream sounded like heaven right now. Some Kahlua on top wouldn't be a bad thing either.

"What do you think, Candy?" Stephen's hand slid down my shoulder.

I jerked, twisting in my seat to look back at him. I also realized we were parked in front of my condo, and the engine was off. Both men stared at me. *Wow, way to zone out, Candy.* I gathered my purse up from the seat beside my hip and reached for the car door. "What do I think about what?"

The siren gave a musical laugh. It was a beautiful sound. "I said...since you're a chef, you must know the best places around here to eat. I'm starving."

"There won't be anything worth eating at the places that are still open this time of night." I popped the door open and set one foot on the pavement.

"Oh." The disappointment in his voice was pretty heartbreaking. It tugged at my soul...everything about these men did. It was the way it was *supposed* to be with mates. Too bad nothing else about this situation was how mating was supposed to be. Stephen sighed mournfully. "That's too bad. Have a nice night, Candy."

Damn it. I squeezed my eyes closed and sighed. I turned back to look at them. "The best place around would be *Chez Candy* then. Would you like to come in for a snack?"

"We wouldn't want to inconvenience you." Michael's blue gaze searched my face.

But Stephen was already hopping out of the SUV. "Oh, yes, we would. She's a chef, I'm headed for a severe case of anorexia, and she's kind enough to offer to feed me."

He gave me big, puppy-dog eyes and a hopeful smile. Michael heaved a long-suffering sigh and rolled his eyes, taking the keys out of the ignition and sliding out to join us on the curb. Pushing a button, he locked the vehicle and gave me a slightly chagrined look. "Sorry about this, Candy. He's incorrigible."

"It's all part of my charm." The siren slung an arm around Michael's shoulders. "You just need to lighten up, handsome."

"And you're just the man to help me with that little job, is that it?" He slanted the shorter man the kind of look that would have set my panties on fire.

"Okay...follow me, gentlemen. No sex on the front stoop please." Executing a quick pirouette, I pulled out my keys to unlock the main door and led the way to my condo. My hands shook a little as I opened my front door. What had I been thinking when I invited them in? I was a crazy masochistic glutton for punishment, that's what. Seriously off balance.

I hustled to put the kitchen island between them and me. Motioning to two of the stools on the other side, I turned toward my fridge and started pulling Tupperware out. "Have a seat, guys."

Yeah, I had a million snacks ready to go...what could I say? Cooking wasn't just a profession for me, it was an obsession. "Are you in the mood for something sweet or something—"

Propping my chin on the top container, I spun back around and found that they hadn't sat where I had told them to. No, both men were shrinking my sizeable kitchen down to claustrophobic proportions. The wolf inside me whimpered, urging me to touch and taste both of them. Michael had his arms crossed and his hip propped against my counter. He watched me with the kind of intensity reserved for a predator tracking prey. But that was ridiculous. I was the only predator here holding back on my wolf instincts for all I was worth. I shivered, liking the idea of him hunting me more than I should.

Stephen reached to take the plastic containers out of my hands, his fingers lingering on my skin. I narrowed my gaze at him, letting the wolf out for a moment, showing the icy eyes and pointy canines. He blinked, but showed no fear. In fact, he looked more...fascinated than anything else. It confused me. I was fighting this and neither of them were helping. Didn't they know what would happen if I unleashed the predator? No, no they didn't. Because they couldn't sense what I sensed. Too many secrets I kept locked inside. Secrets that had become lies, since I never told the people they affected. Michael. Cyn. And now Stephen.

Exhaustion crashed into me, threatening to suck me down into a whirlpool. I watched Stephen set the Tupperware on the counter beside Michael. Leaning in, he pressed a quick kiss to the other man's mouth. Heat whipped through me watching them. I swallowed before I started drooling. What would it be like to watch them do more? To see my mates fuck, bring each other to hot, screaming orgasm? A shudder went through me, and I crossed my arms over my breasts to hide the way my nipples peaked at the thought.

Stephen opened the mascarpone cream and then the strawberries, a hum of pure pleasure rumbling in his chest. When he turned back around to look at me, he held one of the fruits covered in cream. He licked the extra from his fingertips. Michael scooted to the side to give me room at the counter. His gaze swept up my bare legs to my breasts. "I don't think I need any snacks, but *you* look good enough to eat, Candy."

Irritation whipped through me. Why did they insist on teasing me when we all knew they'd never do anything about it? What had I ever done to deserve this kind of torment? True, they didn't know *how* torturous it was, but still... F*uck*. I tried to force a teasing note into my voice. "Yeah. Right. You're all talk and no action, Mr. Lawyer."

"You should tell her." Stephen sucked the cream from the tip of the strawberry, then bit into the red fruit. Fae mischief danced in his green eyes again as he glanced from me to Michael and back.

A warning sounded in the big human's voice. "Stephen—"

"Tell me what?" I arched my eyebrows, wondering what game the Fae was playing. He had flirted and toyed with me on stage, now he did the same off. How would he draw his lover into his sport?

A heavy sigh was Michael's answer as he looked between the two of us. He reached out to wrap his fingers around my biceps, drawing me closer until I could feel the heat of his big body through our clothing. He dipped forward until his nose was a hairsbreadth from mine. I could feel the hot rush of his breath on my lips. My knees weakened, my eyes drooping to half-mast as I swayed towards his tempting self.

"Candy." He stroked his fingertips down my cheek. God, I craved his touch more than anything in the world. "What Stephen thinks I should tell you is...I've wanted you since that first day. Why do you think I've always flirted with you?"

I shook my head, trying to clear the lust. "But...you never *did* anything about it. And I—well, I saw you with a guy once, so I thought you were—"

"Gay? No, I'm more about taking my half out of the middle. Which is Stephen's preference too." He chuckled ruefully, bracketing my jaw with his strong fingers. "But I never touched you because you're my sister's best friend. *And* after all the shit I said about Andre and other magical people, I figured you thought I was pretty much a dick."

I covered his hand with both of mine, sympathy winding through me. "I understood where you were coming from back then."

"Do you still understand?" He leaned even closer, tilting his head until his lips met mine for the first time ever. They were softer than I'd imagined, caressing mine in the lightest brushes of flesh against flesh. Desire fogged my brain, and I forgot why this was wrong, why this was a really bad idea, hell, even that Stephen was eighteen inches away. I *liked* that he might watch this—and he wasn't exactly voicing a protest. Then every sane thought was gone, washed away in the rising tide of longing. I just...felt.

"I understand." My hands dropped to clench in his shirt, and I demanded, "More."

"Yes." His mouth settled over mine to feast. He buried his fingers in my hair, angling my head so that he had full access to my lips. His tongue swept in to tangle with mine. I bit his tongue softly, and he groaned. The kiss grew bolder, wilder. Just like I liked it. His lips crushed mine, and his arms crushed me to him. The feel of his big, muscular body pressed to my softer curves made my excitement boil over. The years of built-up tension broke through the wall of indifference I'd tried to shore up against him. Desperation whipped through me, and I wrapped my arms around his neck, trying to climb him. His hands cupped my ass, lifting me so I could wind my legs around his trim hips. He spun me, pushed me back against a wall of cabinets and rubbed his hard cock over my pussy. Grinding against me, the fabric of his pants stimulated my hardened clit. I pulled my mouth away from his, throwing my head back to cry out.

"Candy." A low groan rumbled in his chest as his lips brushed over my exposed throat. I buried my fingers in his thick hair, holding him close. He opened his mouth and sucked on the tender flesh. My back arched in reflex, trying to get even nearer to him and that amazing mouth. It was too much. My pussy clenched in desperate want.

"Please, Michael. I need you."

"Ah, God, Candy." His palm lifted to cover my breast, stimulating the taut nipple with his thumb. A whimper got caught in my throat when he swirled his tongue up to my earlobe, sucking it into his hot mouth. He bit down lightly and rolled his pelvis against me. An electric jolt went through my body, and I shuddered in his arms. He pinched my nipple, twisting the tip.

Fire flooded my system, and my hips moved in the kind of sensual rhythm I couldn't control. I clung to him, opening my mouth on his neck to suck and nip at his salty flesh. The wolf demanded that I bite down hard. I shuddered, holding back on my instincts to move against him in wild abandon. He pushed his pelvis into mine, working me in the hard, insistent tempo that took me right to the edge of orgasm but didn't allow me to fall over. "Michael, I'm so close. Please, I need more."

"Not yet, not yet." He froze, and I died a little. My claws slid forward and dug into his shoulders. He grunted and shrugged against my hold. I loosened my grip, stroking an apologetic hand down his back.

He startled when he looked at me, his mouth falling open in shock. I pressed my fingertip to my mouth, and I felt my fully extended fangs. My eyes would be icy werewolf blue, the wolf wanting her mate. And my appearance obviously scared the shit out of him. I expected to feel a pierce of regret, but the wolf was too much in control, and I was too far gone to care that he would reject me. Unwrapping my legs from around his waist, he set me on my feet. I nearly cried out again, for entirely different reasons. My clawed fingers flexed and I turned away, not daring to look at him. The emotional pain would come later, when only the woman was left to deal with the hurt.

"That was hotter than I imagined it would be." A strangled note had entered the siren's voice. When I glanced at Stephen, I saw he was stroking his cock through his pants. "And I have one hell of an imagination."

I looked him over, not bothering to hide the wolf this time. They'd come into the wolf's den willingly. If they wanted an apology for my nature, they'd be waiting a long time. Licking my lips, I stepped toward the Fae halfling and reached out to take over the stroking. A low growl soughed from my throat, and the burn in my veins increased.

His hand covered mine, showing me exactly how he liked to be touched. Up, down, up, down. Slow torture. The musky scent of his desire caressed my sensitive nose, his musical groans kissing my ears. Moisture from his bulbous crest seeped through his pants. My other hand lifted to flick open his zipper. His breath caught when I pulled his hard cock out and sank to my knees before him. I wanted him in my mouth, wanted to taste his flesh. A shudder went through him as I slid my tongue along the underside of his dick, working my way up until I could take the head into my mouth. He buried his fingers in my hair, fisting tight as I sucked him deep. His flavor burst over my taste buds, and I knew I would never banish it from my memory. It was embedded in my psyche, and I would know his taste, his scent, his essence anywhere.

The heat that had never abated held me tight in its grip. Stephen's passion fed my own, and my hips rolled to the same rhythm that I sucked him. I closed my eyes and savored every moment of this chance to touch one of my mates. It was too sweet, made me burn too hot. I shivered, my nipples going rock hard. My eyes snapped open again when large hands cupped my breasts from behind. Michael. "You look hot with your mouth stuffed with cock. You know that, right?"

A moan escaped me, his words making lava flow through my veins. My breathing picked up speed, my heart pounding as excitement and anticipation flooded me. His palms slid down the front of my dress until he reached the hem. One hand tugged it up to my waist while the other slipped around to dip into me from behind. The first touch of his fingers on my slick pussy lips made me moan. He pressed them up into my hot channel, setting a fast, harsh pace. I grabbed Stephen's slim hips for balance, still sucking him so deep the head of his cock hit the back of my throat. I groaned, working Stephen with my mouth as Michael worked me with his fingers.

He rolled a fingertip over my clit. His hand angled, and the fingers inside me hit my G-spot. I screamed around Stephen's dick, my pussy convulsing. My sex clenched around Michael's fingers repeatedly, and he continued to thrust into me, to drag it out as long as possible until my breathing became little more than ragged sobs. Stephen's hard cock slid from my lips, and I rested my forehead against his thigh, shuddering and twisting my hips.

Michael's fingers withdrew, and I felt him stand, moving away from me. I looked up when Stephen stepped back to see Michael turning him by the shoulder to face the counter. Kicking Stephen's feet apart, Michael urged the siren forward until his forearms rested on the countertop. My eyes widened as I watched Michael grab the back of Stephen's belt and roughly jerk his pants down. He groaned as Michael stroked over the tight muscles of his naked ass, parting the cheeks to tease his anus. Using his free hand, Michael unfastened his slacks and pulled his long, hard dick out. I sucked in a shocked breath, insidious heat winding through me at the sight of my two mates together. It was the most erotic thing I'd ever seen. Michael inserted one, then two fingers into the siren's ass, widening him to prepare him for penetration. Then Michael pulled his hand back to grasp his cock, nudging it into Stephen's tight pucker.

"Damn, Michael. I want it hard. I need it." He shuddered and groaned between clenched teeth as Michael drew back his palm to slap the siren's backside. I watched Michael's cock sliding in and out of Stephen's anus, and my thighs squeezed together as excitement tightened within me, flooding my core with fire. Even though I'd just come, witnessing them fuck had me right on the edge of orgasm. The scent of them and the musk of sex intoxicated me, clawing at my control. Biting my lip, I slipped my fingers between my legs to stroke the slick folds.

"Don't just watch, Candy. I didn't tell you to stop sucking him," Michael's voice growled, the tone harsh with unspent sexual need. He tilted his head, urging me to join them. A flush of need raced up his handsome face as his hips bucked hard, driving his dick into the siren.

Stephen turned his head to look at me, his emerald eyes glowing with a Fae's supernatural power. Lust pulled the skin tight across his sharp cheekbones. He was right on the edge, and I could help him over. I grinned at him, baring my wolf's fangs. He made a noise halfway between a groan and a laugh, dropping his head between his arms. I moved forward on my knees until I could pump his cock between my fingers. Michael pulled Stephen's hips farther back to give me more room. Rotating my palm over the head of his dick, I curved my hand around the shaft and drew him towards me to suck him between my lips. I extended my claws to curved talons, stroking the edges up and down his cock.

The Fae's body shuddered with the impact of Michael's quickening thrusts. It drove Stephen's cock farther and farther down my throat until I could swallow the tip. My throat contracted, closing tight around his dick. He hissed out a breath, and his hand came off the counter to grip my hair, pulling my mouth away from him. His hard cock danced in the air, and his fingers fisted painfully in my curls as Michael buried himself deep and froze, groaning as he came inside the Fae's ass.

Our harsh breathing was the only sound to be heard, and my body shivered with unsated desire. It was all I could do not to ride my clit on my heel. I burned so much watching them, playing with them both had been so fucking hot I wanted to die. Michael pulled himself free of Stephen's body, and the siren groaned as he sank to his knees. Michael went to the sink to clean himself up.

Reaching out, I couldn't stop myself from stroking Stephen's still-hard cock. "How is it possible you haven't come yet? I must be seriously losing my touch with blow jobs."

His hips arched into my touch, those Fae eyes glittering. But the enchantment in his voice was pure siren. "Gorgeous, the thought of coming inside you was enough to make me hold back. But, damn, you have an amazing mouth. I have to taste."

Threading his fingers into my hair again, he drew me forward until we knelt facing each other. He dipped down until his lips pressed against mine. His tongue swept into my mouth, and our mouths toyed with each other. He bit my lower lip softly, making me moan at the slight pain twining with my intense pleasure. His free hand curled around my ribs to grasp the zipper on my dress. Cool air touched my back as the teeth rasped open, making me shiver. His fingers dropped to cup my ass, pressing me to his hard cock. I lifted my leg, curling it around his hip and opening myself to his penetration. *"Please, Stephen."*

"Sweet little Candy." He rubbed the head of his dick against my pussy. He jerked the hem of my dress up until he could pull it over my head. My breasts spilled free into his palms. I choked on a breath at the first touch on my bare nipples. He lifted them and closed his mouth over the tight crests one after the other. I arched into him, crying out when he bit down. He straightened, wrapping his fingers around my knee and pulling me wider. His emerald gaze locked with mine when his thick cock nudged against me. He pushed me back, yanked his shirt over his head and moved until I was stretched beneath him on the cool tile floor. The heat at my front combined with the chill at my back sent my senses reeling. The soft hair of his chest stimulated my nipples, making me shiver. I moaned when he sank inside me. It had been so long since I'd been with a man that the stretch of it almost hurt. I closed my eyes, clinging to his shoulders.

He chuckled roughly. "Look at me, Candy." When I complied, he whispered softly, his sweet breath brushing over my cheek. "You were seconds from biting Michael, gorgeous. He may not know what that means for a wolf, but I do. And that you're touching me at all now...tells me the secrets you hide."

"Stephen, I—" Tears flooded my eyes and I gasped. How long had I kept the truth to myself? I suddenly felt stripped bare, more naked than I'd ever been. I knew, then, that I'd been right about Stephen in the club. He understood me, my pain and my joy. He understood it all. My mate.

His hands framed my face, and his cock plunged and withdrew in slow, maddening strokes. The tiniest smile played over his sensual lips. "Do you believe in love at first sight, gorgeous?"

I choked on a breath, the tears spilling from the corners of my eyes. "I'm a wolf. With the instincts I was born with, what do you think?"

Wiping the tears away with his thumbs, he let the smile widen. "Mark me."

"I can't take it back if I do." I snapped my legs around his waist, lifting my pelvis into his thrusts. It felt amazing, the pleasure making my wits scatter. I tried to hold myself together, but the woman and the wolf wanted to do exactly as he'd suggested. Please, God, *please.* I wanted him so much, to claim him, to bind him to me forever. Mate, mate, *mate.*

"I felt it at that party with Michael, and again the moment I saw you tonight. I know what I want when I see it." He looked me in the eyes, making it clear that what he was seeing, what he wanted, was *me.*

"Fuck me harder, Stephen." A smile bloomed on my lips, and my claws scored his shoulders.

That musical laugh burst from his throat. "Damn, I love you, Candy."

His hips slammed hard against mine, driving his cock deep into my sex. My pussy spasmed around his dick, making us both groan. He rotated his hips, changing the angle to an incredible penetration. The head of his cock hit me...just right. My head fell back as he rode me hard, grinding me into the floor. Swift and deep, just the way I craved it. It was too good, and I was so close to orgasm. I sobbed because I knew it would end too soon, far too soon. I wanted to stay this way forever, locked in the carnal ecstasy of mating. The deep fire inside me flamed higher and higher, scorching my flesh. Consuming me until I didn't know where one sensation stopped and the next began. Where *he* ended and *I* began. Then I exploded into a million pieces, arching as my pussy milked the length of his cock over and over again until I twisted and shuddered beneath him.

"I love you, too," I breathed, and another tear leaked from my eye. I did love him. The wonder of it seeped into my heart, into the very fiber of my being. It had happened so fast, but that was the way with mates sometimes. That instantaneous connection that went beyond all logic. The connection that was soul-deep from the first instant. I knew it, and so did Stephen.

Perfect.

My fangs sank into the flesh of his shoulder, marking him as *mine*. The blood flowed like sweet nectar on my tongue. I licked the mark until his body locked, until he shouted my name and slammed deep inside me, coming in hot jets. His head bowed and his wings exploded from his back. They flexed, fully extending into what looked like gossamer black dragon wings. The light filtered through them, making them shimmer.

A gasp ripped from my throat. "Beautiful."

"Yes." Michael sat on the floor, propped against a cabinet as he watched our exchange. But now he reached out, stroking a finger along the tip of one wing. Stephen shuddered, snapping them back in. They reabsorbed into his shoulders and he rolled off of me, panting. He threw an arm over his eyes. His thigh relaxed, resting against mine.

Chapter Five

Long moments passed before my breathing began to slow, before my heart stopped galloping. A smile curled my lips, and sweetness ran through me. I yawned and stretched against the hard floor, twisting to get a kink out of my back. "You know...my bed is way more comfortable for laying on. I think it was even designed for it and everything."

Stephen chuckled and propped himself up on his elbows to look at us. His gaze narrowed on Michael. Then he winked at me and whispered out of the corner of his mouth, "Uh-oh. He's thinking again. Always dangerous."

"Hilarious." Michael shook his head, glancing from me to Stephen and then scrubbing a hand down his face. "So...the two of you are mated now. Just like that? Forever?"

"Until we die, yeah." Wariness trickled through me. I'd had humans react to me with everything from titillation to scorn, but my heart tripped at the idea of having my mate turn away from me now that he *knew* what he was to me. He didn't need a werewolf's hearing to have listened in on what Stephen had said to me. Michael was smart enough to figure out the truth. Sitting up, I crossed my arms over my nudity.

Equal parts confusion and uncertainty flashed in his blue gaze. I felt him groping for words, always falling back on the politically correct lawyer when he wasn't sure how to react. "I don't even know how to take this all in. I'm not...what you two are. I'm not magical. I don't have those kinds of powers, those kinds of instincts that tell me who to be with for the rest of my life. Who to love."

I snorted and shoved my hair out of my face. I should have known. It was easy with Stephen. We understood each other, but with Michael? It had always been hard, always fraught with misunderstanding. And years of pain. We had traveled down a bumpy road, Michael and me. "I never expected you to be magical. I wanted you to want me the way I want you, regardless of species or abilities. Magical, human...none of that matters to me. I was born to be with you, to crave you. To *love* you."

"And you can accept that?" His ebony brows drew together. "You don't even have to know someone to mate with them and bind yourself to them for the rest of your life? You met Stephen tonight. You don't know if he's a psychopathic homicidal maniac. You don't know anything about him."

I grinned at him, tilting my head to the side. "You do. And I know you. I trust your judgment."

"Gee, thanks, you guys. I'm really feeling the love." Stephen crossed his legs at the ankles, watching the two of us duke it out with the avid enthusiasm of a sports fanatic.

Michael ignored the siren's sarcasm and kept his focus on me. "That's beside the point. If there'd been no me, if there'd been only him, it wouldn't have changed what you did."

"No, it wouldn't have." I searched his eyes, trying to understand him, trying to make him understand me. I reached out to cup his strong jaw. "You want this to be logical, Michael. You're a human and a lawyer...logic is what you cling to. Love isn't logical. Instincts aren't logical. I *have* to trust that fate wouldn't mate me to a homicidal maniac. I have no choice. I know that means I operate on a different set of principles than you do. It *doesn't* mean one of us is right and one of us is wrong. You can't put my instincts on trial and make a ruling on the matter. I accept you just as you are, I accept that we're different and I cherish those differences. I hope one day you'll feel the same."

"And if I don't?" Confusion still shown in the azure depths of his gaze, and I knew he struggled to accept what Stephen and I simply *knew*. But that was why we both loved him so. He was different than us. We were creatures of instinct, of reaction. He was the balance point for that. We both craved that, craved him. Stephen with his Fae mischief, and me with all the animalistic passion of my soul.

I winced, struggling to hold back the pain of his doubt. He was human, and I loved that about him. Even if it meant that we were constantly at cross-purposes. It made us both reconsider what we knew, what we embraced without question. "I'd accept that too. I would never force you, Michael. That's not how mating works. Not for me, not for any but the most archaic of my kind. I'm just glad you know the truth now. It hurt...hiding it. Hiding *from* it...and you."

He sighed heavily. "I feel like I'm never quite on the same page as magicals, as if I'm always struggling to catch up."

"We'll wait for you," Stephen spoke again, that quiet understanding on his face. It seemed odd from him, and yet it fit. Wise and playful, serious and sweet. The dichotomy of a halfling's soul. "But someday, handsome, you're going to have to take a leap of faith."

Open honesty filled Michael's gaze, blending with a bit of rueful self-deprecation. "It could take years. This is *me* we're talking about. Flirt and fuck around? Sure. Even *love* I can get on board with. Barely. But commit to forever? Believe it can last? I don't know." He swallowed. "I wouldn't change either of you for anything, and I know I need you. But the rest...I'm not sure I'll ever get there. Not even for you."

"We love you, and we'll wait for you. We have to." I pushed myself to my feet and held my hand out to him. He hesitated briefly before accepting it, and I used my superior strength to haul him upright. "And while we wait, I have some ideas about how best to pass the time. *Years'* worth of ideas."

Stephen caught the edge of the counter in his hand and heaved to his feet. Slinging an arm around my shoulder, he flashed his pretty smile. "You know, I really love the way you think."

Chapter Six

Leading the way into the bedroom, I lay back on my king-sized bed and crooked my finger at my mates. The sight of their big, firm bodies, the hard arcs of their rising erections, made the muscles in my belly quiver. They'd both completely stripped on the way to my room, so they were as nude as me. Heat spread through my body, tightened my nipples to stiff points and renewed the moisture between my legs. "C'mere, lovers. Time to test-drive some of those *ideas* of mine."

Stephen pushed Michael towards me. "You first, handsome."

The hot smile on Michael's face made my breath stop in my chest. That I knew now the kind of follow-through that promise carried only made my anticipation peak higher. I'd seen what he'd done to Stephen, and I'd waited a long, long time for a taste of that myself. I was going to get it. My claws raked lightly up the sheets, and I knew my eyes had gone wolfish. He didn't hesitate this time. His lips met mine in that same slow kiss we'd had in the kitchen. I closed my eyes to take in his flavor.

He stroked his fingers over my breasts, tweaking my nipples lightly, teasing me until I wanted to scream. Instead, I moaned into his mouth, mating my tongue with his. The wolf inside me whimpered in delight at being petted. The woman liked it just as much. His hand moved down, grazing my stomach until he dipped into my soaking curls. Fire and ice raced over my skin as he pushed two long fingers into me, widening me for when his cock would replace his fingers. Cupping his hands under my shoulders, he pulled me up until I straddled his muscular thighs, lifting me so he could sink into me all the way to the hilt. Damn, he was thick. It felt so amazing, better than my fantasies had ever painted it. My head fell back, breaking the kiss, and my eyes damn near rolled back in my skull when he rotated his hips, working in at a different angle.

"Jesus *Christ*, Stephen." A deep groan issued from Michael's throat, and I knew Stephen had entered him from the way our bodies jolted from the impact, from the way Michael's thighs widened to spread us both. Knowing we were all connected in the most carnal way possible only increased the dampness between my thighs. Stephen chuckled wickedly, and I couldn't blame him. God, it was so fucking hot.

"Fun, isn't it, handsome?" He bucked his hips, and Michael grunted. Stephen slid his hands up Michael's ribs, curving them around his shoulders to seat him more deeply. It sank him deeper into me as well, and we all groaned. "Me inside you, you inside her. It could be like this forever. Just say the word."

A hiss issued between the human's teeth as he clenched his jaw, arching his back into the siren. "What happened to waiting?"

"I will wait... This is just a taste of how good it could be." And then Stephen started a swift, pounding rhythm guaranteed to push us to the very edge of sanity. Bracing my feet against the mattress, I lifted and lowered myself into each thrust. Michael pumped into me hard, and the slap of skin on skin echoed in the room.

I smiled at Stephen over his shoulder. The Fae groaned, whispering what sounded almost like a song in Michael's ear, "I love you, I love you. Forever, my love."

And I chanted in his other ear, "I love you, love you, *love you.* Michael!"

Michael shouted, each of us wringing him dry. We exploded together, each crying out. Hot fluid flooded my pussy, and I tightened around Michael. Flames licked at my skin, tingles breaking in the wake of the intense heat. My finger's laced together with Stephen's on Michael's shoulders. The three of us, locked together. We shuddered over and over. Michael still thrust into me in short jabs of his cock, and my pussy flexed tight each time. My breath stuttered to a stop, and I arched helplessly. The world blurred before my eyes and became a wash of pure sensation. I treasured each one. The sound of our breaths, the scents of our mingled passion, the heat and fire of *us.*

I laid my forehead against Michael's, staring deep into his pretty blue eyes. "I crave you. I have from that very first day. I will a hundred years from now." I sighed, shivering as the air conditioner kicked on and raised goose bumps on my sweat-dampened skin. "God, I love you."

A rusty chuckle rumbled from his broad chest. "Yeah, I caught that. I also catch it when Stephen says it every day."

"I can't help it that you need a daily reminder, my little skeptic." The siren kissed his shoulder lightly.

He smiled, resting his head back on the siren's shoulder. Soft tenderness entered his gaze as he looked at me. He angled the same look at Stephen. "I don't want to be a skeptic forever. In the courtroom, yeah, but...not with you. I want...I want what Cyn and Andre have. I want to know that there are people who love me and will *always* be mine. In sickness and in health." He swallowed hard and closed his crystal blue eyes for a moment. When they opened, there was no more confusion, no more doubt. Just clear resolve. "I'm ready to take that leap you mentioned. With you. With both of you."

"Well then." The same sweetness that pierced my soul flooded Stephen's emerald gaze, and I knew he'd been waiting with baited breath for months, wanting Michael to make up his mind as badly as I had. Then a Fae smile, full of mischievous light, bloomed on his face. His fingers tightened around mine almost painfully, and I saw them dig into Michael's shoulder as well. "My turn."

A musical note, so clear and pure it almost hurt sounded in my head, built in intensity until it drowned out everything else, until it wrenched at my very soul. Stephen. It was Stephen. A second note joined the first, deeper, richer, and it vibrated through me. Michael. What shocked me was the third note that joined them, lighter, sweeter, almost like the song of a flute. Me. My sound joined them until it all became one note, building and building until my skin shivered with the intensity of it. A siren's song.

Both men started moving again, Stephen in Michael, Michael in me. Like the music, we wove together in a sensual tempo. I watched the Fae's wings unfurl from his back, fluttering as he curled them around us. The music climbed, striking higher notes. Picking up the beat as we moved faster. The press of them against me, the plunge of Michael's long cock inside me, the stretch of my sex around him, the hot scent of sex. Each sensation piled on top of the next, each translating into the symphony in my mind. The music throbbed as I did, reaching for an intense crescendo that had starbursts exploding in my vision. It plunged deep into my soul, lighting me up from the inside out. I screamed, but I couldn't hear it.

Instead of pulling away, I clung to them both, trying to accept, to understand. I threw my head back and howled, the low, keening wail of a wolf. The fetters loosed, and wolf and woman became one...more fully than I'd ever experienced before. They'd given me this. My two mates.

Stephen groaned as he came, the sound almost musical. He slid out of Michael and rolled away. Michael angled his chin up, baring his throat to me. "Do it."

I didn't pause this time, didn't consider if he would regret it later. The wolf was unleashed and I couldn't rein it in. The animal and I had melded together, one purpose, one need, one unstoppable, undeniable craving. My fangs bit deep into the base of his neck, and I drank from him, binding him to me until the day we both died. *Mine.* Every ounce of anticipation that had built up inside me since the day I met him crashed around me, shattering like fragile glass. My pussy clenched, milking his cock as my fangs milked his flesh. He shoved me onto my back, covering me, riding me into the mattress until he came hard and jetted deep inside me. I flicked my tongue over the wound, healing it with the beast magic of my kind. Still I kissed it, sucked it until he screamed for mercy, until I'd dragged every ounce of sensation out of him that I could. Until he knew as deeply as I did that we could never be parted.

"*Candy.* I'm yours, Candy, and you're mine. You'll always be mine." He slumped over me, panting for breath. Sweat slid down his face, sealing our bodies together. His gaze met mine, and he smiled. Worshipful sweetness shone there, the emotion one I was too terrified to put a name to. "I love you."

I broke then, covering my eyes with my hands. A sob choked from my throat and tears cascaded down my cheeks. Using my werewolf strength, I lifted him off of me and rolled out from under him. I curled into myself, hugging myself tight. How long had I dreamed of this moment, of hearing those words from this man? How long had I been sure it would never come? The *years'* worth of agony from denying myself my mate fell away, and it almost hurt it was so good. The sweet edge of relief sliced through me. But now I felt stripped bare, raw from all the emotion that had ripped through me tonight. Stephen. Michael.

"I l-love you, too. I love you b-both," I sobbed. I drew up my knees and curved my arms around them, rocking myself as the tears continued to fall. I couldn't make them stop, a dam had burst inside me and I couldn't hold back the flood. "My m-mates."

"Candy—" Panic edged Michael's voice, the capable lawyer helpless as his hands hovered over my hair without touching. I could sense how close he was, could sense him with every fiber of my being. The connection was intense, overwhelming.

God help me, it was more than I'd ever imagined possible. I was drowning in it.

Stephen slid his hand up and down my back, crooning wordless comfort in my ear until my sobs slowed to rough, gasping hiccups. I shivered, tightening my arms around my knees. I could hear the music in my head still, a soft chime that rippled and soothed my pain. The melody would be as much a part of me as it was him. All the pieces of my soul coalesced in the space of a heartbeat, joined by light and music and magic and...love. A wavering smile curled my lips as the last of the heaving sobs released their grip. My breath hitched in painful spasms, and I shook in wracking shudders. Finally, I sighed and sniffled. Spent. And...happy.

"Here." Michael pushed a tissue into my hand. "Are you all right, Candy?"

"Yeah." I sat up and blew my nose, balled up the tissue and tossed it into the wastebasket across the room.

"Nice shot," Stephen praised. I could feel how he tried to lighten the moment, how he tried to make it easier for me. "Werewolves have the best reflexes. You guys need to start your own basketball league."

"Who says we haven't just taken over the human league in disguise?" I winked at him and gave a watery chuckle.

He smoothed a hand down my calf and kissed my knee. "You're sure you're all right, gorgeous?"

I tugged on one of his brown curls. "Yes, I'm sure."

"Then why were you crying?" Michael's hand rubbed small circles on my back. "I didn't expect that kind of reaction to a declaration of love."

"It was more the buildup and the doubt than the actual declaration." A wry smile touched my lips. "Think of it as years of foreplay."

"Don't scare me like that again." He rested his forehead on my shoulder. "I thought something was really wrong, that I'd totally fucked this up somehow. Already."

"Humans." Stephen heaved a long-suffering sigh—a damn good imitation of Michael's—and flopped over onto his back.

Michael lifted his head to glare at our other mate. "Whatever, fairy-boy."

"Who're you calling a fairy, fairy?" Stephen flicked his hand dismissively. "It's *Fae*, thank you very much."

A wicked grin lit the human's face. His palm curved around the back of my neck possessively. "I'm not *all* fairy."

Equal possession flashed in the siren's emerald gaze, and he wrapped his fingers around Michael's wrist and my ankle. "Me neither...guess that makes us both halflings, doesn't it?"

Michael's broad shoulder lifted in a shrug. "As long as Candy gets the other half, sure."

"Hell yeah." Pure male ego oozed from both of them.

I rolled my eyes, but cupped my palms around each of their jaws. "The two of you are insane, you know that, right?"

"Yeah," both men echoed. Stephen stuck his tongue out and crossed his eyes. "But you love us anyway."

"And we love you." Michael arched an eyebrow, heaving that patented long-suffering sigh at the Fae's antics.

I laughed so long and hard, I had to wrap my arms around myself to hold in the mirth, and still it kept coming. Like the tears, I couldn't stop it. And I didn't want to. This is what pure joy felt like. This is what *belonging* was. I'd been so long without the close bonds of family that the ache of it was wonderful. Yeah, they were crazy. And they were going to drive *me* crazy...for years, I hoped. But this was all I'd ever wanted. Love, contentment, belonging. Now it was mine for the rest of my life. And so were they.

Crazy Little Thing Called Love

Dedication

The usual suspects: Loribelle Hunt, Jennifer Leeland, Eden Bradley, R.G. Alexander, Dayna Hart, Lilli Feisty, Robin L. Rotham and Bethany Morgan.

Chapter One

My brother crooned into the microphone on stage, and I think every female in the vicinity swooned. Oh, who was I kidding? Most of the men too. Stephen Parthon's appeal was pretty universal, and he had both a male and a female mate to prove it. A proud grin curled my lips, but I hid it by taking a drink of my margarita. As a ball-busting music company executive, I couldn't appear *too* much the doting big sister. I had my reputation to protect after all.

"Hey, beautiful." Some drunken troll staggered up, winked and flicked his fingers against my wings, which made my whole body jolt. "Wanna take me flying?"

And I really meant *troll.* Even for his race, he was an especially ugly one. I had to work hard not to wrinkle my nose or slap him with enough fairy magic to *really* send him flying. Attacking him, of course, would get me kicked out of the bar, which I didn't want. "No, thanks. Maybe some other time."

"Okay," he slurred, grinned, and staggered back the way he'd come. At least he was a happy drunk.

I twitched my wings to get the feel of his fingers off them, brushing a hand down my short, sparkly silver dress. Backless, as were most of my shirts and dresses. I loved my wings, so why not show them off? They looked like black and purple butterfly wings, with little inward curls at the bottom that framed my ass. Might as well showcase *all* my best assets right?

Shifting on the barstool, I crossed my legs and propped my elbow on the polished wooden surface that stretched along one side of the renovated warehouse that was the Eclipse bar.

It seemed fitting that my brother's going away show should be here, in a magical bar, where our journey had begun over a decade ago. Stephen's career had skyrocketed during the past year. We'd sold out the world tour within the first week and had to add tour dates. It was a crazy, crazy thing. Not that I was complaining, but I had to stay in L.A. and take care of the business. Someone else managed the day-to-day aspects of Stephen's career now instead of me. It was a good thing. It meant growth for us both. Money. Security. Stability. Independence. Things we craved.

Well, maybe not the independence for him, but definitely for me.

He got that about me though. He'd always had this *understanding* about him that people loved. That and the natural charm and charisma from his mother's siren side and our father's Fae blood made him an unstoppable ball of empathetic energy. People drew to him like moths to a flame. It had only gotten more powerful as his relationship with his two mates deepened. The magic that unfolded between them had balanced him somehow, gave him the emotional stability to really soar. That kind of love, I couldn't give him. He was my *brother* after all.

But I had to admit, deep down in the soft, mushy center of my very cynical soul, that I wouldn't mind a little bit of that for myself. Especially now that he was leaving.

Loneliness was a totally foreign emotion to me. I *preferred* being on my own, and when our father died, I was a nineteen-year-old kid and my seven-year-old half-brother had come to live with me. It had been a rough adjustment for both of us. I don't care what the legal age of adulthood was. At nineteen I was still a kid raising a kid. Going through all the custody rigmarole meant there were so many people telling me what I should do and how I should do it and when and where and what the rules of parenting were and...and...and... It never stopped. I like going my own way and doing my own thing. I crave it, in fact. I need my independence, which is probably why, at thirty-nine, I'd never even had a twinge of desire for a husband or kids.

So, watching Stephen find so much happiness with his mates had been great, but it did remind me that having someone in my life might not be a bad thing. Then again, all the men who'd applied for the position had inevitably tried to control me and simply couldn't accept that I had commitments on my time that I couldn't ignore just because they were feeling needy. I don't mind ties with other people that keep me grounded, but I was born with wings—I *need* to fly.

But Stephen was the one about to spread his wings, and I was being left on the ground. He was poised to do great things and had a career he loved. I had been a part of all that, I had helped him become the truly amazing man he was. Hell, yeah, I was proud. Pixie Dust Productions *and* Stephen Parthon had both become a huge success.

So, now I just got to sit back and enjoy. I'd accomplished a lot and had a whole lot of money to roll in for it. But, Stephen? He was my pride and joy. If I felt a pang that he no longer needed his big sister to look after him, it was soothed by the knowledge that I raised him well enough to look after himself.

"Hey, Pixie." Someone spoke behind me, jerking me back to reality. Turning, I saw one of the owners of Eclipse setting a fresh margarita next to me.

"Heya, Jerrod!" I reached over the bar, clapped my hands over his oh-so-gorgeous face and planted a wet one on his kisser.

He cracked up. "Better watch out, Lena and Rachel are *both* pregnant. The hormones might make them react in ways you can't predict."

"You are a brave man, my friend." I mean, what guy in his right mind had *two* women he was fucking living under one roof with him? But he was a werewolf, and their race didn't get to pick their mates, did they? Fate or instinct or whatever did the picking for them. The fanged races were so odd. I twitched my wings again, just to feel them whisper against my back.

"The hormones also mean they can't get enough sex to satisfy them." Jerrod offered me a sly wink. "It's good to be me, trust me."

I cocked an eyebrow, but couldn't hold back a wicked grin. "Nymphomania by pregnancy. Who'd have guessed?"

His broad, muscled shoulder lifted in a shrug. "Not me, but I find with women it's best not to ask why. That saying about gift horses…"

"I've heard it."

"I've got to run. Enjoy your evening." And then the big werewolf was off serving more drinks.

Taking a deep swig of my cocktail, my gaze went to the other wolf I knew. My sister-in-law, Candy. As far as I knew, she was the only other wolf besides Jerrod to ever have two mates at the same time. It had caused some waves in the wolf pack, but they'd all gotten over themselves eventually.

Then again, neither Candy nor Jerrod was a stranger to controversy. Candy's best friend was a vampire, which was totally *verboten* since the two races had hated either since the dawn of time. Jerrod and his mates had made Eclipse a neutral-territory business long before it was fashionable not to pick sides in the vamp-wolf war. I'd always known I liked Jerrod. The man had sense.

The two groups were pretty much on all the other magical races' shit lists, but Eclipse was open to everyone, no matter whose shit list you were on. Anyone who wanted to start something here—even if it was just to blast some sense into an obnoxious troll—was shown the door. Or tossed out of it. Their choice.

That didn't make Eclipse particularly safe for humans though. No one would try anything inside the bar, but take a walk out to a car or cab and all bets were off. Especially with vampires around, it was like throwing blood into shark-infested waters. The only human with the guts to be here was Stephen's male mate, Michael. But surrounded by his werewolf wife, Candy, his vampire sister, Cyn, and Cyn's enormous vampire husband, Andre, I figured he'd be just fine. I should probably go visit, but I wasn't feeling particularly social tonight.

And since I wasn't Stephen's manager anymore, I didn't have to fake it. There were a *few* perks to being in charge and delegating to others. I took a deep pull on my icy drink, forced myself to set it down before I chugged the last half of it, and winced at myself. I was wallowing just a teensy bit in my lonely self-pity, dreading the morning when Stephen would be gone for four months. This would be the longest kid brother and I had gone without seeing each other in two decades. His mates were going with him, and I was *not* going to play fourth wheel to their unconventional little threesome. So...for business and personal reasons, I was about to be left to my own devices. I knew I preferred my own company, but it was one thing to choose to be alone and another thing to have it forced on me. I'd be over it in a few days, but I wasn't there yet.

Crystal Jordan

What I needed was a distraction. Something to take my mind off the desire to wallow.

A cute Fae who looked only a year or two older than Stephen gave me a wink and a once-over. Not bad. I might have to chat with him later. My gaze moved on as I continued to scan the crowd.

"Well, hel-*lo*." Okay, yum. *This* guy was maybe three feet from me, a little to the left, and facing the stage. The guy was hot enough to make a girl melt just looking at him.

A navy blue T-shirt hugged the heavy muscles of his shoulders and back. And the things his ass did for those jeans had to be illegal. Nice, very nice. I would seriously love to take that ass for a test drive. It would be an awesome way to end my dry spell.

He glanced back at me as if he'd sensed my gaze moving over him. Early to mid-forties, I would guess. Silver edged his dark hair and laugh lines bracketed his eyes. Why men looked better as they aged, I would never know. It was damn unfair. Then again, it did make the view a lot nicer for women than it did for men, so that worked for me. The young Fae was completely forgotten. A man with some experience who knew what he was doing when he fucked a woman would beat out an excited young puppy any day.

That's when I recognized the face. Malcon. The werewolf Alpha. I'd only seen him on the news and in a suit before. He'd looked great, but I wouldn't have guessed he was hiding a body that hot and hard under the Armani.

Good thing I was only looking for a bedmate for the night, because there was no way in hell I'd touch the *Alpha* with a ten-foot pole otherwise. But just for tonight... I offered him a slow grin, which made him lift an eyebrow. Stephen started a new song onstage, and Malcon faced forward again.

166

Not to be deterred, I plucked my margarita from the bar, swished my wings for a light landing as I hopped off my stool and casually sidled up beside the Alpha. "Hi."

"Hello." He offered me a quick smile, but kept his focus on the stage. Obviously, he'd come to enjoy my brother's show, which meant he had good taste.

I didn't know much about the Alpha other than he'd been pretty unobtrusive as an heir, unlike some of the wild hair-up-the-ass heirs in other wolf packs. He'd made waves when he first took the reins by making it clear that no wolf in his pack could engage in the war with the vampires. It meant that violence between the two species had ground to a halt in the short time he'd been in power, at least in our region of the world. I, for one, was in favor of peace.

A shiver slid up my arm when his fingers brushed my wrist. "Let me buy you a drink."

Well, it wasn't exactly a request so I tilted my head and considered. "No."

"No?" His dark gaze flicked back to me and both eyebrows arched.

I motioned to his half-empty drink with mine. "I'll buy the first round."

A low chuckle rumbled from him and his white teeth flashed in a brilliant smile that made him even more gorgeous. "Fine, but the next one's on me."

"Deal." I motioned at Jerrod, who nodded, set two fresh beverages on the bar in record time, and then flicked a wicked look between Malcon and me. I stuck my tongue out at him as I took Malcon's glass, drew a hot little spurt of magic from the air around me, and *zapped* out our old drinks for the new ones.

"That's a handy little trick." Malcon slid one hand into his pocket.

"Thanks."

He swirled the ice in the amber liquid in his tumbler when I handed it to him. "Your brother is amazingly talented."

"He is, isn't he?" I didn't bother to hide the pride in my voice.

The Alpha dipped his chin in a nod and sipped his drink. Watching the muscles in his throat work was outrageously sexy. Jesus, I needed it bad if a man taking a drink was enough to get me hot. Or hotter than I had been already.

Then I grinned as something occurred to me. He shouldn't know I was Stephen's sister. Except for the green eyes, we didn't look *that* much alike. Stephen was tall and muscular to my short and slim, and my hair was stick-straight blonde to his curly brown. "Well, you're the werewolf Alpha, *Malcon*, and you're on the news, but how do you know who *I* am?"

"I asked Jerrod when I saw you at the bar." A little smile played at the corners of his mouth. Well, he was interested. Good. He glanced at me. "I thought it only polite to let you enjoy your brother's show before I came on to you, Ms. Parthon."

"I appreciate that." And I did. How many guys would have even considered that? Nice to know the guy I was going to let take me home for the night was, well, *nice.*

The low beat of a drum drew my gaze to the stage. Stephen's voice dropped to a husky purr, rolling out a love song that had every couple on the teensy dance floor.

"Dance with me, Pixie." Malcon snagged my glass, gave both our drinks to a passing waiter, and then slid his hand into mine.

"I don't—" But he was already pulling me along with him. The Alpha had made a decision, and I got to fall in line. I seriously considered digging in my heels, but since I was the one who wanted to shag him tonight, I figured touching him some more wasn't a bad plan. I rolled my eyes at myself as he dragged me into his arms. And then I didn't give a damn who had decided what because I was plastered from the thighs up against all those hard muscles.

His palm settled at the small of my back, pressing me even tighter to him. If I'd had any doubts about whether or not he was on the same page as I was for how this evening should end, they were laid to rest when I felt the rigid length of his erection digging into my belly.

Heat slid through me like a drug, loosening my body so that I was all but lying on him. He gathered me closer with every turn on the dance floor. His thumb moved in slow circles against my back, edging over the material of my dress to slide across my skin. I arched into his touch a bit, loving the feel of the slight callus on his fingertip. It was stimulating and unexpected in a man I knew worked in an office all day. His wolf's claws scraped ever so lightly against the flesh of my back, and my sex clenched tight.

I sucked in a breath and the hot, masculine smell of him made my nipples harden to aching points. With the next turn, he slipped his heavy thigh between mine. The flex of muscle in his leg when he moved made him rub against my clit. I had to bite my bottom lip to hold back a mew of pleasure. Burying my face against his warm chest, I tried to get a hold of the lust that wound tighter and tighter inside me. Wanting him was one thing, but we were in *public.*

"Oh God." I closed my eyes when that stroking hand on my back touched the edge of my wing. Fairy wings were so incredibly sensitive. A shudder passed through me, and moisture flooded my pussy. "Oh my God."

"Really? That good, huh?" His other hand splayed between my shoulders, his fingers spreading so that he touched the base of both wings. Still, he continued to trace the outline of my wing with one fingertip. My fingers bunched in his T-shirt, and I didn't know if I should push him away or pull him closer. His leg and his hands and his body against mine were going to drive me to madness if I didn't get some relief soon.

His finger swirled into the lower curl of one wing. This time I couldn't stop the whimper that bubbled in my throat. I arched mindlessly against him. "I'm going to come right here, right now, if you don't stop that."

"Let's get out of here." He dropped his hands and pried himself away from me with a low groan of protest.

Suppressing a shudder, I tucked my wings in so that they absorbed into my back. No need to tempt either one of us more than necessary. "I have to say good-bye to my brother."

A look that was equal parts desperation, annoyance and resignation flashed across his face. "How much longer is his show?"

I ran Stephen's song list for the night through my mind and heady relief swept through me. "This should be it. They'll want an encore, but I can sneak in if I go now."

Lust pulled the flesh taut across his high cheekbones and his dark eyes had burned to a savage icy blue. The wolf was fighting with the man for control. "Hurry, Pixie."

I turned on a heel, no longer giving a damn if he voiced everything as a command couched as a request. I wanted him tonight, and I was going to have him. The audience applauded wildly, screaming for an encore as I had predicted. I climbed the short flight of stairs on the stage to grab my brother while he and the band waved and sucked down some water before they started again. "Hey, baby bro. I'm going to run early."

"Okay. I love you, sis." He didn't ask questions, for which I was eternally grateful. Knowing Stephen, he'd probably seen me almost get down and dirty right there on the dance floor. He pulled me into a huge bear hug, lifting me off my feet.

"Love you too." I turned my head to kiss his cheek. "Tell your mates I said good night, will you?"

"Will do." Setting me back on my feet, he grinned at me. "You're coming to the airport to see us off tomorrow, right?"

"I wouldn't miss it." I caught his face between my hands. "I am so proud of you. Don't ever forget that."

"I'm proud of you too." His green eyes softened, and he squeezed my shoulders.

I got a little misty eyed, which was damn embarrassing considering I was headed off to bang a guy I'd met fifteen minutes ago. Ah, well. Shit happened. I wasn't one to question which way the wind blew. I just let it carry me as high as it could and enjoyed the rush. Seizing the moment was what made me who and what I am today. I popped a final kiss on my brother's cheek. "Let's save the mushy stuff for tomorrow."

A laugh that rose like a music scale rippled out of him, following me as I spun back for the stairs. I could see Malcon waiting beyond the edge of the crowd. His eyes had changed back to their normal ebony shade, but that didn't stop the heat that sizzled between us when our gazes met.

When I'd thought he would be the perfect distraction, I had no idea how right I would be.

Chapter Two

Malcon owned a metallic blue BMW Z4. I almost moaned when I saw it—I'd been talking myself out of buying one for months. Shooting him a grin, I waved my handbag at his car. "You realize you're parked in the owner's space don't you?"

"Jerrod's a good friend." He hit a button on his key ring, and the car doors unlocked. Opening the passenger side for me, his dark gaze moved down my bare legs like a caress. I slid inside and let the supple leather seat cup my body. I wanted Malcon pressed that close to me. Closer. I shut my eyes and pulled in a steadying breath, but the ache between my thighs hadn't subsided a single moment since we'd separated on the dance floor.

The car dipped when he got in and closed his door, cocooning us in silence. I opened my eyes to look at him, knowing he'd see my desire and not caring one bit. "How far to your place?"

"Too far," he growled and reached for me.

A laugh startled out of me. "You aren't worried about your Alpha reputation? Someone might see you getting hot and heavy in the backseat of a car like a horny teenager."

While we weren't out in the open, this wasn't exactly a secluded lot. Most people would be watching my brother's show, but there were no guarantees. Malcon grunted. "This car doesn't have a backseat. Come here." A self-deprecating smile curved his lips. "I haven't even kissed you yet."

"I—" His lips cut off whatever I was going to say, and they moved slowly and worshipfully over mine. The man could *kiss*. I slid my fingers into his hair, loving the silken texture of it. He licked my bottom lip, pressing for entrance. A shiver went through me, and I moaned softly. Taking the opportunity to slide his tongue into my mouth, he tilted his head to deepen the angle. Fiery need burned inside of me. His groan vibrated against my lips, and I fisted my hands in his hair, twining my tongue with his.

Malcon jerked away, panting hard. "We have to stop or I'm going to fuck you."

"I wasn't protesting." My body shrieked at the loss of contact. My sex ached to be filled, the emptiness almost painful. My voice was more a demand than a suggestion. "I want more. I want you inside me."

He dropped his forehead to the steering wheel, and I could see him wrestling for control. I had a feeling that he didn't have that problem very often, and it made me grin that I could push him so far, so fast. He'd done the same to me, so it was only fair. He sighed and straightened. "I can sense the people inside Eclipse starting to move. Your brother's show must be over. I spend enough of my life in the spotlight. Some things *are* meant to be private."

Smoothing my skirt, I chuckled. Considering how reporters had crawled out of the woodwork when my brother had taken on two mates, I could sympathize. "Not an exhibitionist, huh?"

"Not even a little." He slanted me a slightly concerned glance. "You?"

What was he worried about? Did he think I was going to magically tie him down so people could watch us do the deed? Ew. I lifted my eyebrows, but shook my head. "Nope."

"Good." A relieved sigh made my brows arch higher.

He turned the key and flipped on the defroster to clear some of the fog from the windows. There was a lot of it. Our kiss had made it beyond steamy in here. The ride to his house was a complete blur as I tried to get a grip on the lust grinding through me.

We pulled into his garage, and he cut the ignition. I stepped out of his low-slung little bullet as the garage door slid shut. Hurrying around the hood, I met him at a door that fed into his kitchen. It was beautiful. I didn't care.

Dropping my purse on the counter, I shot into the living room and looked for a hallway or stairs that might lead to a bedroom. We needed a bed *right now*. He caught my arm, swinging me around to face him. Then his tongue was in my mouth, his hands cupping my head. I jerked at his shirt, pushing it up his chest until he had to break the kiss to pull it over his head. He dropped it without a second glance and had his mouth back on mine with blinding speed. My fingers found his nipple, flicking the flat little disc with my nail. He groaned, filling his hands with my ass to rub his erection over my pussy. Liquid heat flowed through me, and I wanted him inside me. I ached with the need. Wrapping one leg around the back of his, I opened myself as wide as I could in this dress and moved against him. "Malcon, please. I need you."

He froze at my words, and then a great shudder ran through him. I stepped out of my heels while he shoved my panties down my legs. Pulling my dress off, he stripped me quickly. My hands got busy with unfastening his jeans and soon he was as naked as I was. His palms slid over my bare flesh, making me shiver with painful need. His cock branded the lower curve of my belly like a hot iron. The soft hair on his chest rasped against my nipples, stimulating my too-sensitive skin until I cried out.

"Damn, Pixie." He spun me around to face the back of a low leather club chair in front of a huge fireplace. "Put your hands on the arms."

I did. The top of the chair dug into my waist, and I had to stand on my tiptoes, but it wasn't too uncomfortable to bear. At this point, I wasn't even sure I'd notice if it were. My body was close to the boiling point, and the supple leather warmed beneath my palms. Malcon's thigh nudged mine open. His palms slid up the backs of my legs until he reached my ass cheeks. Prying them apart, his finger swirled around my anus and I shuddered, my hips already moving.

"Later." His voice held dark promise. He wrapped his hands around my waist and pulled me into a heavy thrust that seated his cock all the way to the hilt.

I sucked in a shocked gasp and my inner muscles flexed and stretched around him. "Oh my *God.*"

He worked his dick inside me slowly at first, but quickly picked up speed and force until his thighs slapped against mine. The hot drag of his flesh in mine made me dig my nails into the chair's leather. I could feel my own moisture running in beads down the insides of my legs. A soft laugh spilled out because it felt so damn *good.* This is exactly what I'd needed tonight. Him.

His hand smacked my ass hard, and I heard the sound echo in the wide room. It made my lungs seize and my pussy clench. He groaned. "You're so damn tight, Pixie. You're killing me."

"What a way to go, right?" I flicked a glance over my shoulder at him and winked.

A chuckle rasped out of him. His palms cupped my ribs, pulling me upright. The angle wasn't quite as good as he thrust into me, but the feel of him pressed to my back was a sensual delight. His finger began to work my clit in swift, rough

175

motions, and I decided I liked this angle just fine. My hips moved to shove back into his thrusting cock and then forward again to keep contact with that maddening finger. His mouth dropped to suck and kiss the side of my throat and heat whipped through me to dampen my sex even further.

Wrapping his arms tight around me, he froze with his thick cock buried deep inside me. His fangs scraped against my neck, making me choke in desperation. His soft lips brushed my skin as he spoke. "Tell me to bite you."

I arched, the heat inside me hot enough to scald. My nails raked down his arm, but there was no way I could overpower a werewolf without hurting him with my magic. That would stop what we were doing and I only wanted him to *move*. "Please."

"Please, what? Tell me." He licked my throat before he dug his fangs in a little deeper, and the pleasure-pain almost made me come. God, I needed to come.

Twisting in his arms, I damn near sobbed. "Bite me, Malcon. Make me scream."

His fangs sank deep, his cock hammering into my pussy as I came so hard my legs collapsed underneath me. He caught me in his strong arms, still working that thick cock inside me. My sex spasmed around his dick, milking the long shaft in hot pulses that made me moan loudly. He sucked and licked my throat again and again, the sensation enough to make my eyes roll back in my head. Jesus, the man could fuck like no one I'd ever known before. It was the last thought I had before I passed out from the overwhelming ecstasy.

Chapter Three

I woke up sprawled face down on Malcon's bed. Bright sunbeams filtered in through huge windows, and I winced and rolled over to bury my face against his chest to block out the light. "Jesus Christ. Buy some curtains."

He grunted and sifted his fingers through my hair, making the tips brush against my shoulders. "Good morning to you too."

"What time is it?" I was *not* lifting my head to face the light of day until I absolutely had to.

There was a pause and the muscles in his arm and chest flexed under my cheek as he shifted to look. "*Shit.* It's almost nine. I have a meeting in an hour."

"Shit!" I bolted upright and scrambled for the edge of his mile-wide mattress. "My brother's plane takes off soon. I have to pick him and his mates up from their place and drop them off. Where are my clothes? Shit, shit, *shit!*"

He got a nasty glare from me when he snickered. "Scattered in the living room, I believe. I'll drive you home."

"You have a meeting." I looked back at him as I reached his bedroom door.

His broad shoulder lifted in a shrug, and he flipped open a closet door. "One of the few perks of being the Alpha is they can't start without me. I don't abuse the privilege, but that doesn't mean it's not there."

I chuckled on my way out the door, hustled down the stairs and stuffed myself into my dress and shoes. By the time I remembered I'd left my purse on the kitchen counter, Malcon was on his way downstairs, his jacket and tie draped over one arm while he fastened the cuff of his shirt on the other wrist. He was even better looking in the light of day, while I was pretty sure I looked like road kill. I was too afraid to ask if my hair was standing on end. He might tell me the truth.

His ebony gaze slid over me, lighting with appreciation, which was nice but probably not saying much about his taste in one-night stands. I preceded him out into the garage where he held the door open for me again. I could have protested, but that would have taken time I didn't have. He was on his side, in the car and backing down the driveway in under a minute. That's when I got a good look at his house. His palatial house. And I'd been in music stars' homes, so I knew how monumental they could be. I was usually uncomfortable in them—a throw back from growing up middle class—but I hadn't been in Malcon's home. Then again, he'd been distracting me just the way I'd hoped he would.

Braking at the light at the bottom of the hill, he flicked a glance at me. "Where to?"

"Take a left." In a miracle I wasn't about to question, L.A. traffic was obscenely light this morning and Malcon had me at the curb in front of my beach bungalow in record time. I might even be able to squeeze in a shower before I had to go pick up Stephen.

Malcon shot me another inscrutable look. "Do you like Italian?"

It took me a moment to process that, so I blinked at him stupidly. "Are you asking me to have dinner with you tonight?"

178

"Among other things." He grinned wolfishly. "But, yes, I want to have dinner with you."

Heat wound through me at the naked desire in his gaze. Okay, I'd only planned on a one-night distraction, but I was going to have some free time with my only family out of the country. What could it hurt to have a full-fledged affair with a man who made my toes curl? I wouldn't mind a regularly scheduled orgasm that didn't require batteries. Reaching into my purse, I pulled out my cell phone and flipped it open. "What's your number?"

He rattled off the number, and I punched it in. His pocket vibrated, and he fished out his cell. "Okay, your number popped up on the caller ID. I'll give you a ring when I get off tonight."

"Great, then we can both get off." His rich laughter followed me out of the car and I had to hustle to get ready, but I had to admit I was a hell of a lot more chipper about the coming months without my brother than I had been the night before.

I had chosen well when I picked Malcon over the young Fae at Eclipse.

I should have chosen the young Fae over the Alpha. What the hell had I been thinking? This was like some kind of sick, twisted joke. I'd walked Stephen, Michael and Candy into the airport for our little kiss and cry time, said good-bye, and been on my way out when one of the flat screen TVs they had constantly playing the news flashed my picture. That wasn't completely unheard of, especially if they were discussing Stephen's world tour, but the words that scrolled underneath my photo made my mind whirl.

Local werewolf Alpha finds his mate, music producer Pixie Parthon.

More words went by and Malcon's picture flashed beside mine, but I'd seen all I wanted. More than I wanted, in fact. I was *no one's* mate. I didn't even want to get married. A few people turned to look from me to the screen and back again, so I spun on my heel and walked out to the parking garage, growing angrier and angrier by the moment. Why would Malcon release a statement like that to the press? This was ridiculous. I slammed into my car as a thought made ice water flow through my veins. Malcon had bitten me last night. Not unusual when fucking a fanged race, but those bites didn't leave a scar like a mate mark would. My hand shook as I flipped down the mirror on my sun visor and pushed my hair aside to see the side of my neck.

There was a scar. He'd marked me. Rage exploded inside me and I closed my eyes, letting my hair fall into place. There was no way in fucking hell that I was going to give up my hard-earned independence to be the queen of the wolves. And it was really sweet of him to mention he thought *we were mated* when he asked me to dinner. *Thanks so much, jackass.* I revved the engine on my car, left the parking lot in the dust and was a block away from Malcon's office before I realized where I was going.

I still hadn't managed to quell my anger. Oh, well. He was going to get it now.

Fifteen minutes later, my three-inch heels pounded a staccato beat on the marble floor of the huge building that housed the international organization owned by the wolf pack. It was a good thing I was wearing my usual backless blouse today because I was so pissed I couldn't have kept my wings in if I tried. The air crackled around me as I moved, and everyone in the vicinity either turned to stare at me or jumped out of my way. I somehow doubted I'd have that kind of effect on the

Alpha, which just pissed me off even more. The wolf would be lucky if he didn't come out of this neutered.

A bony woman leapt to her feet when I entered the reception area of the pack leader headquarters. Her welcoming smile deflated when she got a good look at my face. "Ms. Parthon. What a surprise. Can I—"

I heard the low, sexy timbre of Malcon's voice coming through an open doorway and I walked toward it. The receptionist gasped and babbled some protest, but I ignored her. I was not giving Malcon a chance to refuse to see me. He was dealing with me right now. Period.

Storming into the room, I didn't even pause when I saw a huge meeting was taking place. Men ringed a long conference table with Malcon at its head. He had a look of calm control that reminded me how out of control I felt, which did nothing to improve my mood.

"Pixie." He was on his feet the moment he spotted me and every other person in the room leapt to follow suit. His gaze cut to the woman trailing in behind me. "It's all right, Martha." His gaze returned to me. "What can I do for you?"

I tilted my head to the side, widened my eyes and propped my hand on a cocked hip. "Gee, I don't know, but did you hear the local werewolf Alpha was mated last night? I saw it on the news. I wanted to come and congratulate you."

And that's when it hit him just how pissed I was. I watched the realization flash in his eyes, but not a flicker of emotion crossed his otherwise contained expression. He looked at me while he addressed everyone else. "Gentlemen, give us the room. Now."

I'd never seen werewolves scatter and scurry so fast in my life. It would have been more satisfying if it hadn't been Malcon who made it happen.

He sat back in his chair, steepling his fingers and pressing them to his lips as he regarded me for a long moment. I thought a small smile quirked his lips, but it was gone so fast I couldn't be sure. "You certainly know how to make an entrance."

"What can I say?" My smile was saccharine enough to send him into sugar shock, and I gave a delicate shrug. "I'm in show business."

He sighed and dropped his palms to the table in front of him. "I'm uncertain why you're upset about our mating. Want to give me a hint?"

"I had to find out about it on the *news*, Malcon!" I threw up my hands and started pacing back and forth in front of the table. My wings swished every time I turned. "You have to be kidding me."

"Why are you surprised? I asked you before I bit you." Standing, he approached my end of the table cautiously, as if I were some kind of rabid animal.

I snorted and folded my arms, which drew his dark gaze to my breasts. "I've been bitten by werewolves and vampires during sex before."

His eyes closed as awful realization crossed his handsome face. He swallowed hard. "You don't need to be having sex for a mate bite to work. It's not like a regular bite anyway. It's a magical marking."

"I got that when I saw the scar on my neck. That was definitely not something I've had before." Like a magical STD I would never be able to get rid of. I nearly snarled at the thought. He had no right to rope me into something like this. Being wolf queen had a million strings attached, and I'd only been looking for a one-nighter. How had *this* happened? "This can't be real. I'm going to wake up any moment, I know it."

He sighed and opened his eyes. "I thought you were willing, but...we *are* mated."

"According to you and your kind, maybe. Not to me and mine." I fluttered my wings for emphasis.

His gaze sharpened. "How do the Fae mate?"

"That's none of your damn business, but it sure as hell doesn't involve shoving your *fangs* into someone's *throat*." And my sex throbbed at the mere thought. I hated the consequences on a major level, but I'd had an amazing time. Damn it.

"You sure as hell weren't complaining about it at the time." His eyes narrowed as he propped his hip against the table ledge and folded his arms.

I arched an eyebrow at him. "At the time, I was more worried about the other part of your anatomy you were shoving into me."

He snapped back, "I can put that part back in if it'll make you happy."

Yeah, I was *not* letting my mind go there at all. That's what had gotten me into this in the first place. "No, what would make me happy is to undo this mess."

"We're mates, Pixie." Regret softened his gaze. He shoved his hand through his hair, sifting the light smattering of silver with the darker strands. "We're meant to be together. I sensed it."

Sucking in a deep breath, I tried to be reasonable about this. "Look, I get the whole mating instinct thing with wolves. In the abstract, yeah, but I get it. That doesn't mean I have to go along with it like some helpless little sheep."

"Does that make me a wolf in sheep's clothing?" He snorted.

I pointed to his jacket and smirked. "Well, it does look like you're wearing a wool suit."

"Ha. Ha." He rolled his dark eyes, and I had to fight not to laugh. This was not a laughing matter.

I paced another little circle in front of him. "Hey, you brought it up, not me."

"Pixie—"

Stopping, I rubbed my fingers over my suddenly throbbing temples. This just couldn't be happening. It was surreal. I shook my head at him. "Look, just stop it okay? This isn't what I want, and Alpha or not, you can't force me to want it."

The look in his eyes gutted me. I wanted to take it all back, to soothe that heart-wrenching pain from his dark gaze. Instead, I forced myself to turn away. One night of sex—even *great* sex—did not obligate me to be his little woman. If I'd thought the other men in my life wanted to tie me down and control me, I could only imagine what an alpha male *Alpha wolf* would do.

Thanks, but no thanks.

Chapter Four

I worked late that night, as if to prove to myself that I was not bothered at all by this Malcon issue. It was business as usual for me. A knock sounded on the front office door and I glanced at the clock, quarter to eight. My assistant had gone home hours ago. Who could possibly be at the door?

I really should have suspected Malcon, but I was stunned to see him when I exited my office and spotted him standing outside the big glass window that looked out onto the elevator bank and hallway. For a split second, I considered leaving him out there and ignoring him, but the Alpha was...alpha, stubborn and persistent enough to harass the building's maintenance staff to let him in. Or, hell, he was a werewolf. He could just break the door down if he wanted and not even break a sweat.

Damn fanged people. Damn alpha males. Damn it.

Flashing him a dirty look, I walked up to the door and flipped the big lock. His grin was nothing less than wolfishly predatory. Moving with that startling speed of his, he pulled the door open before I could change my mind and lock it. Smart man.

As soon as the door swung open, I smelled Chinese food. My stomach rumbled, reminding me I hadn't eaten since the bagel I'd inhaled on my way to pick up Stephen and his mates.

"You have food." My tone was almost an accusation, but it was annoying that the man was a walking temptation on every possible level.

"I thought I should come bearing gifts." Malcon shifted the jacket he had draped over his arm to reveal a black cloth grocery bag for me to peek into. His discarded tie was stuffed in there with the containers of delicious-smelling food.

I looked back up at him, crossing my arms. "How did you know I was still here?"

"Oh, come on. You don't really expect me to reveal my sources, do you?" The smile he gave was enigmatic.

I snorted and didn't bother to favor him with a verbal response. He stepped through the door, and I had to either end up plastered against him or get out of his way. Deciding discretion was the better part of valor, I moved aside and locked the door behind us. He followed the light from the reception area into my office and I trailed behind him, not really sure what to do at this point. I'd never had a one-night stand get out of hand before. That's why they were *one-night stands.* Not that I'd had that many, but enough to know this was *not* normal.

While I hovered near the door, he sat on my couch and set the little white cartons on the glass coffee table. Then he dug out a couple of sets of disposable chopsticks and offered one to me. "Have some lo mein, it'll settle you."

"I'm settled enough," I grumbled, but my stomach was about to eat itself now that it realized there was food in the vicinity. I plucked the chopsticks from his hand without touching him, snagged a container of fried rice and sat cross-legged on the floor next to the low table, glad I'd worn slacks today. He slid off the couch and sat on the floor across from me. Our knees brushed, and I ignored the sizzle of awareness that went through me.

He speared a potsticker with one chopstick. "How was your day?"

"Fine, except everyone wanted to ask about my mating." The smile I gave him was acidic.

Sighing, he winced. His voice was soft. "I'm sorry, Pixie. I thought you felt this connection too. Maybe not to the level that I did—*do*—but I hope you'll believe I thought you were willing."

"I believe you." The expression on his face was beyond sincere. "That doesn't mean I'm willing now or that I ever will be. I'm not even willing to consider it."

"Why not?"

Because he sounded genuinely curious rather than pissed off or offended, I answered him. "I don't do fetters. I don't like to tie myself down. I did it for Stephen when our dad died, but that wasn't a choice. Not really. He's family. But *choosing* to tie myself to one man or one place for the rest of my life? I can't imagine how that would make me happy."

"There could be a guy out there who will give you the freedom to be yourself." He offered me a carton of noodles and exchanged it for the fried rice. His gaze met mine for the briefest moment. "He might even like you just the way you are."

We both knew he wasn't talking about *some guy* in the abstract, but Malcon in particular. I swallowed, smiled and winked playfully. "Nah. Such a paragon of virtue and tolerance doesn't exist."

He laughed and let it go. A sigh of relief whispered out of my throat. The undercurrents running through this conversation were enough to drag me under, but I had to resist the pull. Sighing, I set aside the food, my stomach turning. Tension made knots of the muscles in my neck and when I rubbed them, I hit the mate mark and jerked at the touch on such sensitive flesh. My body reacted and it made my stomach twist tighter. I wasn't afraid of Malcon, but I didn't like the pressure to be something I wasn't, to accept something I hadn't chosen for myself. My business didn't run itself, and I couldn't afford to lose focus. *This* was the life I'd chosen for myself, not being some Alpha's mate.

I looked over at him and saw that he'd stopped eating as well. I offered a weak smile and pushed to my feet. "Don't stop on my account."

"I'm finished if you are." He rose with me, and I felt his gaze on me as I walked over to pack my briefcase and purse. "Let me walk you out."

"That isn't necessary, but thanks for dinner." I glanced up to see that he'd approached while I wasn't looking and was within arm's reach. That made me nervous. "It's not like this is a date or anything."

Stepping well into my personal space, he lowered his head until his mouth was a hairsbreadth from mine. "Yes, it is."

"And you're not getting laid tonight." I narrowed my gaze at him, but there wasn't an ounce of conviction behind my words.

His breath brushed over my lips. "That's a shame."

"Malcon…"

"Pixie…" His voice was a low rumble that made my insides melt.

I tried to put a little more power behind it this time. "I'm not kidding."

"You can't blame me for trying to change your mind, can you?" He gave me a brilliant, beautiful smile and winked. "You would do the same."

I cracked up because he was right, and he caught the sound of my laughter in his mouth. Pleasure crashed over me so fast I gasped, and he plunged his tongue between my lips. I quivered with indecision for all of a millisecond before I twined my fingers through his hair and met his tongue with mine. A hot rush of sensation swamped me tonight as it had last night. I hadn't just imagined how good it had been, but this time it felt so much more meaningful.

Nothing and *everything* had changed since last night, and it freaked me out so badly I pulled back. My body screamed a protest at the loss of contact, and I squeezed my eyes closed. Malcon's hands cupped my hips, and I could feel every impressive inch of his cock through our clothing. I wanted him inside me again, but my mind warned that it would just complicate everything. Lust sluiced through me in a hot wave when he moved one hand around to my ass and the other up to palm my breast. I whimpered and broke under the force of a need that was far stronger than my willpower to resist. Really, how much more complicated could it get?

He scraped a claw over my nipple and the additional slide of my silk blouse over my breast made me sway toward him. Moisture dampened my sex, and it clenched on an emptiness that I knew he could fill. My breath sped to little pants, and I stared up at him. "I want you."

"I know. I can smell how wet you are. The scent of you is beyond intoxicating, Pixie." He groaned and slid his palm around to the open V of my shirt. His mouth met mine in slow, drugging kisses that only whetted my craving for him. His fingers slid over my back where my wings would be if I let them out. I had to concentrate not to have them break free. Fire licked at my flesh everywhere he touched me and goose bumps shivered in the wake of the flames.

My hands slid over him, too, moving without direction from my mind. Up the ridges of his ribs, around his shoulders, down the muscles of his back until I cupped his firm ass. He jerked against me, shuddering at my touch. I felt his cock expand where it pressed into my belly. God, I needed him inside me, needed the hot glide of his hard flesh within my wet flesh. He eased my blouse over my head and had his hands on my bare breasts before it hit the floor. I tugged his shirt out of his slacks. I wanted him naked *now*.

"*Off*," I demanded, and the universe answered. A hum of magic and Malcon's clothing lay in a wrinkled pile at our feet.

He blinked. "Holy shit."

I didn't bother responding, and instead busied my hands with touching as much of him as I could reach. I almost sobbed on a frustrated breath when he set his hands on my shoulders and held me away from him. "Now, Malcon. No teasing."

"What do you think I'm trying to do? I can't do that naked magic thing." Hell, I wasn't even sure *I* could do it again, but the naked magic he *could* do worked well for me. He spun me around and bent me over my desk the same way he had with his chair last night and relief wound through me. He didn't bother trying to undo the complicated clasp on my belt, just used his werewolf strength to pop the thick leather in half. Then he reached around my waist and unfastened my pants. He shoved my slacks down and I stepped out of them and my heels.

"Damn." He spun me around to look at me. His dark gaze burned my body as he took in my thigh highs and total lack of any other underwear.

I caught my lower lip between my teeth and shifted from foot to foot. Shyness wasn't natural to me, but I had to admit I was a bit unnerved by the intensity of his stare. It was a little worshipful and a lot possessive.

He lifted me off my feet and set me on my desk, the cool glass against my overheated skin making me arch in reflex. "Lean back."

I fell back on my elbows as he pulled my ass to the very edge of the desk. Grinning at me, he draped my ankles against his shoulders, and ran his tongue around the very edge of the lace on my stockings.

The lace rasped on my sensitized skin and his breath cooled the moisture his tongue left behind. I shivered and moaned, "Malcon."

"I can't wait, baby. I'm sorry." He sank into me in one slow push, his fangs bared as he growled low in his throat. His dark eyes had burned to ice blue, the wildness within him peering out at me.

His gaze locked with mine, and I couldn't look away. I felt more naked than I ever had in my life, my heart hammering. Some connection had snapped between us that hadn't been there before. I refused to let my mind define it, but it made the sex deeper, more intense than it had been. He started moving inside me, his movements hard and fast and deep. The angle was perfect, the way he held my legs made him hit just the right spot inside me to have me quivering on the orgasm within moments. Still, I couldn't look away from his eyes, and I could see the pleasure there, the way he savored my reaction, the way he didn't hide anything from me. Gone was the cool man in the boardroom this afternoon. *This* was the real Malcon, half-untamed and all wolf. It was a fucking turn on that he didn't play games with me. I loved it, wanted more of it, moving with him as he moved within me.

"I'm going to come," I gasped.

"Thank *God*." He slid one hand down my leg and stroked my clit in time with his deepening thrusts.

Sweat beaded on my skin, making me shiver. Contractions thrummed in my sex, building until I couldn't hold back any longer. My torso arched off the desk, and I cried out his name.

My sex clenched around his cock so hard it was almost painful, the ecstatic rush obliterating everything except *him*.

"Pixie," he breathed, closing his eyes as he came in hard jets of fluid. He swallowed, leaned forward to brace his hands against the desk and let my legs fall to the sides. His gaze met mine, the irises ebony again. "How can you just walk away from this, Pixie? It's too good."

I sat up and cupped his jaw in my hands. He leaned into my touch, his gaze softening in a way that made my insides tremble even though I knew they shouldn't. I sighed and shook my head. "What am I going to do with you?"

"I'll tell you what." His hand slipped up my back to tangle in my hair. "Let me see you for say, a month, and give me the chance to change your mind about the mate thing. If not—no harm, no foul. It'll give me the opportunity to figure out what I'm going to tell my pack in the meantime."

"What do I get out of it?" I tilted my head, shivering as the movement made his fingers slide through my hair.

He pursed his lips as though thinking hard, then he smiled and arched an eyebrow. "Orgasms on call."

A giggle bubbled out before I could stop it. The thought of having an Alpha at my beck and call was laughable, but the thought of Malcon at my beck and call made the laughter fade as a throb of renewed heat went through me. It wasn't a bad deal. I knew he wouldn't convince me to be his queen, but I liked him enough to want to help him out with buying time to come up with a suitable explanation for his pack. It was startling to realize I did like him, even after so short an acquaintance.

I bit my lower lip and narrowed my gaze at him. "There's no crying foul in this offer, right? You won't consider me going out with you or sleeping with you as leading you on when I say no in the end?"

"*If* you say no, then no." He dropped a quick kiss on my mouth, sucking my lower lip between his teeth. "I'm going into this with my eyes open and so are you."

"Then you have yourself a deal." I leaned back, held my hand out for him to shake and watched that little smile of his play over his lips as he folded his fingers around mine.

Then he reeled me in until I was pressed flush against him, and we both groaned. His cock thickened and he thrust it to the hilt within me again, his mouth descending on mine.

I stopped worrying about the future to enjoy the moment with the sexiest man alive.

Three weeks later, Malcon was still on the campaign and gaining ground, I had to admit. I was nowhere near giving in, but every moment I spent with him made me like him more, want him more, *crave* him more. My heart jumped when I saw him each evening, and it saddened me to leave him every morning. I counted the hours to when I got to see him again like some teenager with her first crush.

It scared the shit out of me.

I should call the deal off, tell him no, and move on with my life. I knew it. I'd even tried to make myself say it more than once. So far, I was pathetically unsuccessful. I didn't *want* to stop seeing him, and that complicated the shit out of everything. That was exactly what he wanted. The problem was, things were going smoothly. Nothing had been tested and crumbled under pressure, so it was all shiny and pretty and new. I wasn't running from coast to coast like I had so often. Wolf pack politics and business were good. *We* were good. When the brown stuff hit the fan and splattered the way it inevitably did, he would try to fence me in the way every other male had. So, while I was letting myself enjoy the moment, it was with the slight dread in the pit of my stomach of waiting for the other shoe to drop.

Sucking in a deep breath, I refocused on the quarterly reports in front of me. I had a boatload of meetings tomorrow, so I had to get a bigger boatload of paperwork done tonight. I should be relieved by a break from Malcon, but I wasn't.

An hour later, my cell phone vibrated across the surface of my desk and made me jolt. My heart raced, and I pressed my palm to my chest. I pushed the button on my cell phone that transferred the call to the Bluetooth in my ear. "Hello?"

"Hey, Pixie."

A smile automatically curved my lips at the sound of his voice. "Hey, you. What's up?"

"Not much." I could *hear* an answering smile form on his handsome face. "How late are you working tonight?"

"Late." I looked at the stacks of paperwork that covered every available surface in my office. I sighed. "Very late."

He hummed sympathetically. "That's too bad."

"What are you doing?" I leaned back in my chair and kicked my heels up onto the desk, crossing my ankles.

He chuckled. "Working very late. We're taking a break for another forty-five minutes, but then I have to put in a conference call to Tokyo."

"Ouch. That's what, a seventeen-hour difference?"

"About that, yeah." There was a short pause. "So, I was thinking we should have dinner together."

"If we're both working madly on opposite sides of the city, how do you—" A knock sounded on the outer office door. "Hold on a sec."

My eyebrows arched. Was it him again? My sex clenched at the mere thought of what we'd done together the last time we were in my office. I hopped up to open the door. A courier stood there with a plastic bag from my favorite Italian place in one hand and a vase with a dozen purple roses in the other. I blinked for a moment, then flipped the lock and opened the door. "Hi."

"Pixie Parthon?" The kid offered a bashful smile.

I nodded. "That's me."

"Sign here, please."

I scrawled my name on the digital pad he held out to me, and then collected my booty. Locking the door behind the courier, I couldn't stop the stupid smile that spread as I smelled the roses.

Malcon's voice sounded softly in my ear. "Did you get it?"

"*Yes.*" A little laugh spilled out, and I carried the heavy crystal vase and food to my office. Clearing off one of the piles of paper from my credenza, I set the roses in the middle where I could see them from my desk. I couldn't resist taking another lungful of their spicy sweet scent. "Malcon, the flowers are beautiful. Thank you."

His voice deepened the way it did when he was pleased. "So, like I said, I think we should have dinner together."

"You had Moretti's delivered to you too?" The stupid grin widened with delight. This was without a doubt the most creative non-date I'd ever had. Okay, so it was the *only* one, but still. It was nice of him to think of this.

I heard him shift the receiver against his ear. "They make the best veal parmigiana."

Plopping myself into my chair, I opened the bag and all the various containers inside. There was even a little bottle of Pellegrino. My stomach gave a rumble as I ripped open the packet of plastic silverware. "Mmm, I love their three-cheese ziti. How did you know?"

"The manager told me your favorites."

"Ha! Rosa is the best." I forked a bite of it into my mouth and moaned. "Oh man. This is so good."

His low growl filtered through the phone, and I moaned a little louder on the next bite to torment him. He laughed. "Minx. I'm glad you like it."

"I do." I sipped the fizzing water. "I was going to skip dinner, so this is fabulous. Thank you."

"You're welcome." I heard him chew a bite slowly and swallow. "So...how was your day?"

"Good. Busy." Settling back in my chair, I spent the rest of his break chatting with him about how our work had gone.

It was...nice. I really, really liked it. Almost as much as I liked *him*. I groaned when I hung up the phone, dropping my forehead to my desk. God, I was in so much trouble with this man.

Chapter Five

After a quick dip in the ocean the next evening, I had to jog dripping wet through my bungalow to open my front door for Malcon. Huh. It was unusual for him not to call before he showed up. Shadows smudged under his eyes as if he hadn't slept well. I hadn't slept well without him last night either.

I sighed and shook my head. So. Much. Trouble.

Stepping back so he could come in, I locked the door behind him. Taking a deep breath, I said the words that were going to test this thing we had going on. "I have to tell you something that's not going to make you happy."

"Save it for later then." He pulled me into his embrace, mindless of my wet bathing suit but careful not to crush my wings, to bury his face in the crook of my neck. I sighed and relaxed against him, closing my eyes. It was nice having his arms around me, comforting and secure. I wasn't eager to have the coming confrontation, so I ran my hand down his back, turning my head to kiss his ear. His chest rumbled in a chuckle. "Thank you."

I smiled against his temple. "You can thank me for a lot more in about fifteen minutes."

"Honey, I've been better than fifteen minutes since I *was* fifteen." We both chuckled, but shock made my breath catch when his mouth latched onto the bite mark he'd left on me that first night. Heat flashed from the mark straight to my sex, and I was wet and aching in moments. He plucked open the strings around my neck and ribs that held my bikini top on, baring me to the waist. He cupped my breasts, chafing my nipples roughly.

I jerked at the buttons on his shirt, unfastening the first few. "Take this thing *off.*"

"What, no naked magic today?" But he leaned back, grabbed the bottom of the offending garment, and ripped it over his head to toss aside. Then I had my hands all over that broad chest of his. I hummed with pleasure...the man was a tactile smorgasbord, all crisp hair, silky flesh, hard muscles, and soft, flat nipples that tightened under my fingertips. I flicked my tongue over one, just to show him I noticed his reaction. But I wasn't in the mood for teasing. It had been far too long since he'd thrust his sex into mine, and I wanted him desperately. My fingers fumbled with his pants, jerking open the belt and zipper until I could pull his cock out. My wings whipped through the air, lifting me off the ground so I could wrap my legs around his waist.

"Tuck these in," he whispered, running a fingertip around the curl in one of my wings. I whimpered at the throb that went through my body at even that light touch. My legs tightened around him, and I ground myself against his hard length. A rough sound burst from his throat. "*Pixie.*"

I actually had to concentrate on the simple act of pulling my wings in, but the moment I did, he backed me up against the nearest wall. His claws shredded my bikini bottom and he ripped it away from my body, tossing it over his shoulder. Tilting my pelvis, I made it as easy as possible for him to slide that hard cock inside me.

He plunged into my pussy, stroking hard and fast until I was screaming out an orgasm. I'd never come so fast in my life, and my sex clenched around him so many times I thought I'd die. "Malcon!"

He groaned and went rigid against me. "*Jesus*, Pixie."

"You didn't come?" I whispered, then rolled my eyes at the stupid question. Of course he hadn't. He was harder than blue diamonds inside me.

"Not yet. I didn't want it over too soon." He jerked out of me, panting hard, his arms so tight around me I couldn't breathe.

I raked my nails down his biceps. "To hell with the fifteen-minute rule."

"That wasn't what I was talking about." He laughed, the head of his cock rubbing against my slick flesh. I moved with him, trying to take him inside me. He lifted me higher against the wall, shoved his hips forward, and pressed against the recess of my anus. *This* we hadn't done yet. My lungs seized and I had to fight to keep my wings from bursting out the way they sometimes did when I was this sexually stimulated. I didn't want to do anything that might make him stop, and dark pleasure insinuated itself into every muscle of my body. He pushed into my ass slowly, but his width and length made the stretch sting so bad I had to bite my lip. My nails dug into his broad shoulders. To push him away or pull him closer, I didn't know.

"Is this okay?" he murmured.

Yes. No. I didn't know. I clenched my teeth. Jesus, it hurt. He was huge, but it felt amazing too. "Oh my God."

He hadn't moved a muscle, letting my body adjust to his thick cock. "Should I stop?"

"No." My head rolled against the wall as I shook my head. "Don't stop."

He didn't pull out, just nudged himself inside me. Tiny strokes made me shudder at the sensations that went rocketing through me. One of his hands braced under my thigh, hitching me even higher on the wall, changing the angle of his penetration. I moaned, a tear sliding down my cheek at the pleasurable pain. His other palm closed over my breast, brushing my nipple gently. It tightened under his touch, adding one more sensation to those swamping my system. Sweat beaded on our bodies, sealing us together. I wriggled against him, clenching my inner muscles around him. A snarling growl ripped from him and he thrust faster within me. "Pixie, you feel so damn good. You always do. I love every second with you."

"*Malcon.*" Wrapping my legs tighter around his waist, I tensed my thighs to move with him. We both groaned at the additional friction. Soon he was plunging deep and hard into my ass, and agony and ecstasy blended into one unstoppable force within me. I could do nothing but close my eyes and *experience* it all. Malcon's voice, Malcon's hands, Malcon's hot scent and Malcon's cock stroking into my ass. God, it was so good.

My nails burrowed deeper into his shoulders, and I could feel how close I was to coming. Just a little more, just a few more thrusts, and it would all be over. My head fell against the wall, and my body bowed hard as an orgasm crashed through me. I screamed when his mouth closed over the mate mark on my neck, contractions holding me tight in their grip and each movement of his mouth sent another wave rolling through me. "Malcon, Malcon, *Malcon!*"

He hammered into me, all fetters letting loose as he sought his own orgasm. The look on his face was nothing short of savage, fangs exposed, eyes crystal blue. He threw back his head and howled when he came deep inside me. He collapsed against me on the wall and I held him close, rubbing a hand up and down his sweat-dampened back. I kissed the side of his neck and sighed.

Flicking my gaze to the clock on my living room wall, I smirked. "That was *not* more than fifteen minutes."

He barked a laugh, wrapped me into a tight hug as he lifted us both away from the wall, but didn't let me down. He nuzzled my neck and his bite mark, making that hot-sweet melting start in my muscles. "It's not my fault you came so fast. *Twice.*"

"We need a shower and then a bed." I arched and moaned as he sucked the mate mark, my sex fisting. "Hurry."

He didn't. He made love to me slowly, kissing, licking, and nipping every inch of my body until I begged for more. The man was relentless. All night long. And reminded me every time fifteen minutes went by. When he set out to make a point, he really dedicated himself to the task. I don't think I'd ever come that many times in a single evening in my life.

It was to *die* for.

But the next morning, I knew I couldn't put off the confrontation any longer. I had to get on a plane in a few hours. Sitting up in bed while he lay beside me, I propped myself against my headboard, tucked the sheet under my armpits, and folded my arms. "I have to go out of town."

"Where to?" He didn't so much as bat an eye, leaning on an elbow to kiss one of my crossed arms.

His lack of reaction confused me, but maybe he just hadn't processed this yet. I braced myself, dread sinking like a lead ball in my belly. "To the New York office."

"Okay." He nodded, his dark eyes calm and steady when they met mine. "Give me a day, and I'll have my assistant clear my schedule for as long as you need."

Now I *knew* he didn't get it. Sighing, I tossed aside the sheet, climbed out of bed and jerked on a robe before I turned to face him again. "Don't be ridiculous. You're the L.A. pack leader, so you need to be in L.A. While I'm in New York, I'm going to be working flat out. I wouldn't be able to see you for more than a few minutes a day."

He sat up, the sheet pooling around his waist. "Pixie—"

"I mean it, Malcon." I wrapped my arms around myself protectively, knowing that we'd finally gotten to the part I always hated. This was why I didn't do complicated or committed when it came to men. It never ended well for anyone. "This isn't a vacation for me, and I'm not going to take you with me just to abandon you in a hotel room for days on end. You'd be pissed at me for ignoring you, and I'd be pissed because I told you so."

Emotions flickered across his face so fast I couldn't identify them. "You don't want me with you."

"It's not like it's forever. I'll be back." Some desperate, stupid little part of me prayed he'd understand, that he'd be *different.* "My work never ties me to one place."

"I didn't say a word about tying you to anything. I offered to come with you. And since when have I *ever* acted put out by your work? I have work of my own I could take with me. The pack can live without me for as long as I need it to, and, frankly, I'm an adult and I don't need you to entertain me. This is about trust, Pixie. No matter what I say or do, you don't trust me not to cage you. You don't trust me. You don't want me with you, and we're done here." His mouth opened as if he was going to say more, but he didn't. Instead, he left me gaping behind him, unable to take it all in as he shoved himself out of bed, strode into my living room, picked up his scattered clothes and disappeared.

Just as I'd thought, it was over. I don't know which shattered me more—that I'd never see him again or that it was my fault. Clamping a hand over my mouth, I refused to let myself cry and I forced myself to pack, get on a plane and leave him behind.

Chapter Six

I ached. Every moment of every day for the next month. I had to cast spells over myself to make myself sleep. Still, I never felt rested and exhaustion pulled at my very bones. My soul bled every time I thought of Malcon, and no matter how often I'd told myself it was best that I not have someone tying me down, I couldn't make the pain subside. Whether I liked it or not, I was attached to him. Hell, if I was really honest, I'd admit I was more than attached. A few more days and my work would be done here, then I'd be back in L.A. But I knew without a doubt he would never settle for the easy arrangement we'd had before. I'd ruined that. He would want all or nothing. He would want my trust. Everything.

Could I do that? *Trust* that he would be what I needed him to be? I didn't know, but I also knew I didn't want to be without him. But what did *he* want? I wasn't the easiest person in the world to deal with, and most of the time I was okay with that. But was Malcon okay with that? Did he regret our time together? Did he wish he'd resisted marking me that first night?

Lying in bed, I stared at the ceiling of my hotel room. I was trying to catch a nap before I had to go to a party tonight and pretend to have a good time. Again.

My cell phone blared a loud version of one of my brother's songs. I rolled over and snagged it before it vibrated itself off my nightstand and onto the floor. The number on the display wasn't one I recognized, but had a California area code. My heart leapt. *Malcon.* Stabbing the connect button, I pressed the phone to my ear. "Hello?"

"Hi...Pixie?" A masculine voice that wasn't Malcon's answered. "It's Jerrod."

I frowned and checked the display again. "Hey, this isn't the Eclipse number."

"No, I'm not at the bar. I'm on my cell."

"Oh, okay." I kicked the blankets aside and crawled out of bed. "What can I do for you?"

A long pause fuzzed through the line and I could almost hear him wrestling with how he wanted to say whatever he had to say. "To be honest? You can get your ass back to L.A."

That startled a laugh out of me. "What?"

He sighed. "Look, I know you're Fae and not a wolf, but this thing with Malcon—"

"Jerrod, I adore you, but this isn't something you should stick your wolfy snout into."

He made a rude noise. "That's what Malcon said before I left his house."

I checked my watch. It was three in the afternoon on the West Coast. And it was only Wednesday. "Why isn't he at work? Is he sick?" My voice caught a bit as I asked it, and worry coursed through me.

"Not exactly. That's what I'm trying to tell you." I heard him take a breath before he launched into an explanation. "When wolves are mated, they can't go without their mate long term. A couple of days, maybe a week max. But you've been gone more than a month. I mean, if you die, it's different, the connection is cut, but you're alive. He's still bonded to you."

I thought about it. We *hadn't* gone more than a day or two without being together the entire time I was in L.A. "I'm assuming when you say 'can't go without' you're not talking about sex."

"No, I'm not. I'm saying Malcon is suffering on a level you obviously don't understand because I know you're not cruel enough to do this to anyone deliberately."

Closing my eyes, I felt a harsh pang ricochet through me. What a horrible gamble Malcon had taken when he only gave himself a month to change my mind about mating with him. It sounded as if he was paying an even more horrible price for losing. I forced the hardest question I'd ever asked out of my throat. "Is...is he dying?"

"I don't know." My belly cramped tight at Jerrod's answer. "I've never seen what happens if a wolf goes long enough without. Most of the time, I'd expect the wolf to track his mate down, but Malcon doesn't want to force you."

A breathy laugh escaped me, tears welling in my eyes. "Stubborn ass."

"I called him worse before I left a few minutes ago." I could all but feel the wolf's frustration vibrating through the phone. "He's not hearing it. I've never seen him like this. So, just come put him out of his misery, okay?"

Now it was my turn to sigh as I sank on the bed and dropped my face into my palms. My voice came out muffled. "It's more complicated than that."

"I don't doubt that." Jerrod didn't bend an inch, his tone steely. "But I *do* doubt Malcon's going to hold on to his sanity much longer unless you get on a plane to California and find a way to work something out between the two of you. He's not a bad guy, and he doesn't deserve what he's going through."

"This isn't my fault." Oh, yes it was. I hadn't made him mark me as his mate, but I had left him behind on principle. Guilt pounded through me. Guilt and pain and misery and loneliness that was crippling. What the hell was I *doing*? I didn't have to live like this. I could put *both* Malcon and me out of our misery if I wanted to. I could have him forever if I was willing to take a risk on him, *with* him. I imagined living every single moment with Malcon, and then I imagined living without him as I had for the last month, hording all my independence and sharing none of my life with anyone. No contest.

The truth hit me, and I realized that I loved him. And what *wouldn't* I risk for love? I closed my eyes and let the sweetness of that realization flow through me, soothing the ache in my soul.

Jerrod made an impatient noise. "It's not about blame or responsibility, Pixie. It's about species and biology. It's about a good wolf hurting a hell of a lot because his mate isn't here. Whether you want to be his mate or not, you *are*."

"Thanks for calling." And I hung up on him and whatever else he might have said. Jerrod wasn't who I needed to be talking to.

Malcon was.

He didn't answer my knock, but when I tried calling him, I could hear his cell phone ringing inside the house. He never went anywhere without that thing. He was as bad as I was about always having it with him. So, he was home and he just didn't want to see me.

My heart seized on the next thought. What if Malcon really was dying because I had abandoned him? What if I was too late? Pressing my palm over the lock on the door, I concentrated hard.

"*Open*," I whispered fiercely. The air shimmered around my hand, golden sparks of magic flashing. Fairy dust. It came from the world around me, flowing through me as I called upon it, manipulated it the way my kind did. I heard the lock click and smiled in triumph.

Pressing on the door latch, I stepped into his living room. "Malcon?"

He sat slumped in the chair where we'd made love that first night, staring into the crackling fire. Even though my heels clicked on the hardwood floor and I knew he should have been able to smell me from a mile off, he gave no indication he knew I was there. Concern pumped through me, making my heart trip hard against my ribs. I discarded my jacket on the coffee table and hurried over to kneel beside him. Still, he didn't move, but I could see his face. Shadows cast dark circles under his eyes and lines bracketed his mouth.

"Malcon?" I set my hand on his arm, and he jerked, finally looking at me.

He blinked slowly several times as though just waking up from a deep sleep. "Is this a dream?"

A tremulous smile curled my lips. "No, I'm really here."

"That's...good." His gaze returned to the fire.

I blinked, and my concern kicked up to real panic. I understood now what Jerrod had said about Malcon losing touch with reality. I had to get through to him. Just coming here hadn't done it.

Well, there was one easy way I knew to make a connection with Malcon. It had never failed us before. I stood, hiked my skirt up and straddled his lap. He startled, his palms cupping my hips automatically.

My hands balled in his shirt. "Malcon, look at me."

His gaze snapped to mine, his fingers bit into my flesh and the return of sanity sharpened his ebony eyes. "Pixie."

"Hi, there." I tried to make my smile bright, but it crumbled almost as soon as it formed. I swallowed, so relieved that I hadn't driven him crazy that tears welled in my eyes. Clearing my throat, I looked down. There was so much I needed to say, to explain, and as many times as I had practiced the words in my head on the plane ride from New York, my tongue just wouldn't work now that the moment was upon me.

He gathered me as close to him as humanly possible and buried his face in my throat. His big body shook, and I could feel his tremors running through me as well. "*Pixie.*"

"I'm here. Shh. I'm here." I slid my fingers into his soft hair and rocked him, telling him over and over again that I was here. It was good to be back in him arms. Tears slipped down my cheeks, and I was shaking as badly as he was.

He groaned like an animal in pain, but eased his grip on me to look at me. "For how long?"

"As long as you need me." I wiped my damp cheek on my shoulder. "I'm sorry I left you, sorry I hurt you. I'm here for as long as you'll have me."

A shudder rippled through him and his tone darkened, his eyes flashing to blue and then back to black. "You don't want to make that kind of offer."

I met his gaze, cupping his strong jaw in my hands. "Yes, I do."

"Even though my answer is going to be 'I need you forever, Pixie'?"

"Yeah." I nodded to emphasize the word and grinned.

He sucked in a breath, closing his eyes. "Pixie, you're killing me."

"Literally." My palms tightened on his jaw, and the grin died as guilt ripped through me again at the deep grooves bracketing his mouth, the hurt stamped on his face.

Opening his eyes, he searched my face. "I didn't want...to be like all the other men. I didn't want you to feel guilty about leaving, didn't want to cage you or change you. I want you just as you are. I wanted you to be willing. I thought you were that first night, I really did. And I'm so sorry."

"I know." Stroking my fingers down his cheek, I leaned forward to rest my forehead on his and gave him the whole truth, gave him all of me, gave him what he deserved. "I love you. And loving you changed me, changed what I needed. You didn't cage me, I did that myself by not recognizing what I felt for you. I locked myself into the same pattern I've followed with all the other guys. That wasn't your fault, Malcon. You didn't do anything wrong."

"I marked you when you didn't understand what I was doing. I should have made sure." Regret darkened his midnight gaze, deepening the lines beside his mouth. "But I fell for you fast. Even without the mating instinct, I'd love you for the rest of my life."

A laugh came sputtering out and it tangled with a sob. I was so relieved I hadn't ruined this beautiful, precious connection between us that I had to blink back more tears. "Why? I'm pushy and rude and a pain in the ass."

"You really can't guess?" A smile lit his face.

"No." I shook my head and shrugged. No other person I'd met besides my brother had ever managed to live with me for more than a few months at a time. "I like myself just fine, but why would you *want* to put up with it?"

"For so many reasons." He pulled me tighter against him, and the passion that always sparked between us flared to life as the heat of his hard cock burned through our clothes. That little smile of his I loved played over his lips. "I'll give you a list if you do the naked magic thing."

"Does the list start with the naked magic thing?" The corners of my mouth twitched, but I pinched my eyes closed, set my hands on his chest, one palm over his heart and drew the magic into myself, forming a picture in my mind of what I wanted. Warmth flowed through my limbs, and suddenly I could feel his skin under my fingertips. When I looked at him again, we were both nude.

He laughed. Really, truly laughed, and the last of the shadows fled his face. I smiled at him and moaned when his long cock filled me slowly. He moved gently underneath me, as if to savor every moment. His palms slid up and down my back, his dark gaze caressing my face as though trying to memorize the contours. "You said once that you raised Stephen because there wasn't a choice. He was family. That's what being the pack Alpha is for me. It's duty. I find it fulfilling, but it doesn't bring me joy. *You* do that, Pixie. You're funny and sweeter than you like to pretend. You don't play games, and you have zero tolerance for bullshit. You have no problem getting in my face when you're upset about something I've done. Do you know how refreshing that is for someone in my position? You're like a breath of fresh air. I can be myself around you, and you like me that way. You like that I don't play games either, that I don't try to dick you around."

"You think so?" Emotion banded my chest until I couldn't breathe. This man understood me better than anyone ever had before, maybe better than I understood myself.

"I know it." Fire burned through me as we arched together, his cock stretching my sex with each thrust. Still slowly, but we'd soon lose control and explode together. I couldn't wait. His palms curved under my ass, pulling me tight to the base of his cock. "I can see it in your eyes when we're together. We make

Crystal Jordan

each other laugh. I didn't have anyone in my life like that before you."

"What about Jerrod and his mates?"

"When push comes to shove, I'm still their Alpha." He shrugged, rolled his pelvis to change his angle of penetration, and I had to work to keep hold of the thread of our conversation. I knew it was important, but *damn*, the things he could do to me with his body.

"T-true."

He paused in his movements and I gripped his shoulders, snapping my gaze to his. "When I can feel my duty getting a little too heavy, you remind me to laugh. I *need* that. I need *you*. I don't want to tell you how to live your life. I just want to be a part of it. I want you to *want* me to be a part of your life."

"I do want that. I want you." And I could prove it to him. Offering him a wicked smile, I sank on his hard cock and made him clench his jaw. "Remember when you asked me how Fae mate?"

"Yes. I remember every moment I've ever spent with you. Even when we were arguing." His eyes widened as the implication of my question hit him, and his fingers bit into my flesh.

I gathered the magic to me, felt it skip and dance like golden lightning around my arms and down my body as it grew in strength and power. Then I pressed my palms to his cheeks. My wings burst from my back to flutter madly, and I could see in his eyes a reflection of the glowing magic in mine. His breath caught, but he didn't try to pull back. Instead, I saw wonder there, and he leaned into my touch.

God, I loved this man.

Pushing the magic forward, I arched my hips into his and he followed my lead. Our gazes locked and we moved hard and fast, his hard belly slapping against mine. The carnality of it was beautiful, left me gasping for breath. I could see love and trust in his eyes, and I let him see mine. The depth of emotion made the sex better for me than it ever had been before, even with him. His eyes burned ice blue, the wolf and the man giving me what I needed. Every time he entered me, my walls closed around him, and I could feel the Fae magic building higher and higher inside me until it was almost painful. I gave him a little more with every swift stroke, but I wouldn't be able to contain it much longer. I didn't want to. I wanted to bind him to me, meld our souls until he was mine and I was his. Forever.

He pulled me closer to him, ground his pelvis against my clit, and my control snapped. My power slammed into him full force, filling him as he filled me. A low howl issued from him. His hand fisted in my hair, jerked my head back, and he sank his fangs into my throat again, exactly where his original bite had been. I screamed and we came together, bodies and souls twining in the magic of both our races. My sex milked the length of his cock, but neither of us stopped. A sob wrenched from me as another orgasm exploded through me and another was right on its heels. It went on forever and ended far too soon. I collapsed against him, spent. His fingers stroked through my hair, pulling my head up until our sweat-dampened foreheads pressed together and we stared in each other's eyes. Tiny sparks of gold flickered in his eyes as my magic pulsed through him.

"I love you, Pixie. I love you so much—I have since the first moment I saw you." The naked vulnerability on his face was something I knew no one but I would ever see. "Fight with me, get mad at me, I don't care, but never leave me again. Never."

"I won't. I can't. I love you, Malcon." Tears slid down my face and I held him as tightly as he held me, needing to be as close as we could be. The connection that cycled between us, binding my soul to his, would grow stronger and stronger every day for the rest of our life together. And the craziest thing about it was that that sounded just perfect to me. There was nowhere in the world I would rather be than right here in his arms. I'd meant every word I said. Loving him hadn't caged me, it had set me free, free to fly as high as I could go, free to be myself as I never had been with anyone else before.

Free to love and be loved.

About the Author

Crystal Jordan began writing romance after she finished graduate school and needed something to fill the hours that used to be eaten away by homework. Currently, she serves as a librarian at a university in California, but has lived and worked all over the United States. She writes paranormal, futuristic and erotic romance.

To learn more about Crystal please visit www.crystaljordan.com. Send an email to Crystal at crystal@crystaljordan.com or join her Yahoo! group to join in the fun with other readers as well as Crystal! http://groups.yahoo.com/group/crystal-jordan

GREAT CHEAP FUN

Discover eBooks!

THE FASTEST WAY TO GET THE HOTTEST NAMES

Get your favorite authors on your favorite reader, long before they're out in print! Ebooks from Samhain go wherever you go, and work with whatever you carry—Palm, PDF, Mobi, and more.

SAMHAIN
PUBLISHING ltd

WWW.SAMHAINPUBLISHING.COM

LaVergne, TN USA
03 June 2010
184815LV00001B/88/P